*A*
*Harlequin*
*Romance*

OTHER
*Harlequin Romances*
by VIOLET WINSPEAR

Many of these titles are available at your local bookseller, or through the Harlequin Reader Service.

For a free catalogue listing all available Harlequin Romances, send your name and address to:

HARLEQUIN READER SERVICE,
M.P.O. Box 707, Niagara Falls, N.Y. 14302
Canadian address: Stratford, Ontario, Canada.

or use order coupon at back of book.

# THE SILVER SLAVE

by

VIOLET WINSPEAR

HARLEQUIN BOOKS     TORONTO
WINNIPEG

Original hard cover edition published in 1972
by Mills & Boon Limited, 17 - 19 Foley Street,
London W1A 1DR, England

© Violet Winspear 1972

SBN 373-01637-9

Harlequin edition published November 1972

Printed in Canada

1637

# CHAPTER ONE

THE road was uphill and rather uneven, and only the deep upholstery of the car saved Rosary from being tossed against her companion each time the driver swept them around a precarious bend or through a cobble-paved village. The country through which they drove was scenic and eye-catching, and many of the houses had a Moorish look, while others were set within gardens ablaze with tropical flowers, amid great arching trees and vines that tumbled over old and tawny walls. There was a sense of history, a tinge of magic, a rampant charm to Vozes do Mar.

To imagine the island was not the same as seeing it, and even the vivid descriptions of Lola Cortez, who was a resident, had not prepared Rosary for the excitement she felt as she gazed from the windows of the car and came fully alive to the fact that she was here and actually breathing the fabulous air of this Portuguese island.

Lola, a friend of the Governor, had travelled from Lisbon with the English girl, who was on her way right now to become tutor to his young daughter, who was fifteen years old and an only child. Lola talked on gaily about the *palacete*, the official residence of Dom Duarte de Montqueiro Ardo. She and her brother, who was an artist, lived in a villa close to the small palace and they were received by the Dom, and the Latin girl obviously admired him.

'Often we are invited to dine, and sometimes there is a reception and very smart and titled guests come by private plane from Lisbon and it is all very exciting.'

Lola paused and played a moment with a soft black glove. 'Sometimes Duarte seems a little distant, but that is expected.'

Rosary gazed enquiringly at the Portuguese girl, whose lively dark eyes flashed over her, taking in her simple suit of pearl-grey, and the rather tense way her hands were clenching her soft handbag.

'You seem suddenly much fairer here on the island ... almost alien, and not much older than Gisela herself.'

'I'm exactly five years older than my prospective pupil,' Rosary smiled, albeit a little tensely. Never before had she been described as alien, but here on Vozes do Mar she was the stranger whose looks the islanders would find a little strange. The brilliant sun, she knew, would make her hair seem ashen.

'That makes you twenty!' Lola exclaimed, her eyes looking denser than ever in the deep cream of her skin. 'I know the Dom told Dacio, my brother, that he hoped to acquire a *sensible* woman for the tutelage of Gisela. Sensible!' Lola broke into a laugh. 'At the age of twenty it is not possible, unless one is a wife. You know, of course, that Portuguese men expect sense and sensibility in their wives?'

'Most men probably expect it,' Rosary said drily, 'but I wonder if they always have their hopes realized? What sort of a person is the Dom's wife? I imagine she is beautiful?'

'She was beautiful.' The laughter faded from Lola's eyes. 'Did you not know ... did he not explain in his letter to you that Gisela is motherless?'

Rosary caught her breath in surprise. Somehow she had not connected the Governor of Vozes do Mar with widowerhood. She had pictured a gracious hostess for the *palacete*; a woman so busy with her duties that she

6

could not teach Gisela herself the attributes of being entertaining and well-read. The Dom in his letter had merely said that Gisela had been away at school in a convent but had become so homesick for the island that he had decided to employ a tutor for her ... and being so very Portuguese, Rosary had added in her own mind, he had not fancied placing his daughter in the hands of a male tutor!

'One takes these things for granted,' she murmured. 'How sad for him, and the young girl. Has it been ... long?'

'Since Gisela was nine.'

'And I imagine he couldn't help but give in to her homesick plea to leave her school in Portugal.'

'He can be thoughtful,' Lola fingered one of her pearl earrings, 'but he can also be very much the autocrat. I suppose you are feeling nervous of meeting him?'

'Rather more so than before,' Rosary admitted. 'I expected to deal with ... has the palace no woman in charge of things?'

'Yes, his Aunt Azenha is the holder of the household keys and she sees to the smooth running of the domain, but she is without the authority to choose a teacher for Gisela. I believe she would not have chosen you.'

'And why not?' Rosary looked a trifle indignant. 'I have been trained in music and language by Courland Bell, and it was this fact alone which qualified me in the opinion of Dom Duarte.'

'Your surname is Bell!' Lola looked inquisitive.

'Exactly!' Rosary broke into the smile that slowly revealed a deep, sweet dent at the left side of her softly curved mouth. 'That great old man is my grandfather, and there are few good singers today who have not been taught their art by Cibby, as I call him. I men-

7

tioned this fact in my application for this post——'

'But did you also mention your age?' Lola asked, a trifle wickedly.

'No ... but does it matter?'

'It might. Portuguese people are very circumspect and it might be thought a little more than daring for so young a foreign girl to be living under the same roof as our eminent Governor.'

'You mean...?'

Lola inclined her dark, pretty head, with the glistening curls caught back at her nape by a tortoiseshell clip. 'You are not young enough to be thought a schoolgirl, and not old enough to be thought a *duena*. You are not plain enough, either, to be thought harmless.'

'Whatever harm could I do?' Rosary laughed scornfully. 'I'm not a man-chaser, and my only intent is to do a good job and make Gisela like me. I have no designs on the ... father.'

'You may change your mind when you see him. From his head to his heels he is a man to notice. When one calls him Your Excellency the words have meaning!'

Rosary gripped the soft bag in her lap even harder, for not at any time had she thought of her future employer as a man unfettered by a wife, and she knew enough of the world to know that even in England a single girl under the roof of an attractive widower stood in danger of being gossiped about. It was the way of life, and she hoped to goodness that she had not come all this way only to be found unsuitable because she was young. Oh, why had she not mentioned in her letter that she was twenty? Because Cibby was now eighty the Dom must have concluded that his granddaughter was a spinster lady!

8

'Look, we are turning in through the boundary gates!' said Lola.

At once Rosary was on the alert for her first glimpse of the stately home in which, she hoped, she would be living for a while. Her initial excitement was now replaced by a certain apprehension, and Lola did not alleviate it when she tapped on the glass partition separating them from the driver and asked him to drop her off at a turn in the drive, a tree-shaded one leading through the gardens and lawns of the *palacete*.

'Come all the way with me,' Rosary pleaded.

Lola shook her head. 'No, it is better that you arrive formally. Dom Duarte merely asked me to meet you in Lisbon. He did not suggest that I present you to him.'

Rosary bit her lip and studied the face of the other girl. 'I begin to think that Portuguese people are a little ... ruthless,' she said.

Lola smiled, even as she opened the door beside her. 'You may be right, Rosary Bell. You may indeed find that our charm has running through it a fine thread of steel. Perhaps that is why we have some things in common with the British, eh?'

'Perhaps.' Rosary watched as Lola stepped from the car with grace and took from the driver the overnight case which he had stowed in the boot for her. 'We will meet again, I hope?'

'Of course,' said Lola. 'Unless the Dom decides to be ruled by convention instead of innovation. All the Portuguese I have ever known have preferred that nannies and companions for their children be on the mature side. But good luck! I shall hear soon enough whether or not he sends you packing.'

'From whom?' Rosary looked enquiring. 'Who will tell you?'

9

'Dacio, of course. He is working at the palace, restoring the paintings and portraits in the picture gallery.' With a wave of her hand Lola departed along the path that led, presumably, to the villa in which she and her artistic brother lived. Rosary sank back in her seat as the sumptuous car proceeded on its way, and she felt beneath the shell-pink of her blouse the fast beating of her heart. Taking this job had seemed like an adventure, now all at once she realized the setbacks and complications involved in dealing with people of Latin blood.

They might in some ways be like the British ... as they had been during the reign of the Victorians!

Amused by her own thought, she gazed at the back of the driver, smartly uniformed, with his peaked cap squarely on his dark head. He was formal and polite, and not by the flicker of an eyelash had he betrayed surprise at conveying to his master a fair stranger who looked as if she needed a *duena* herself.

Cibby, the old dear, would have been a little amused. He had taught her not only to love music but to be independent and proud and ready for all that life could offer. From a child she had been with him, for her parents had been in Hungary on a concert tour when there had been an uprising and their hotel had been shelled. From a child she had learned so many things from him and behind her slender façade, her look of youth, there lay a warm, responsive heart and a quick mind.

'Yes, by all means go to Vozes do Mar,' Cibby had said. 'Everyone should live on a tropic isle at some time in their lives.'

And here she was, and when she glanced from the car window she saw that high walls had taken the place of the shade trees, and over the walls hung tangles of flower, cloaking the stone in colour and giving off scent as they passed a tumbling sleeve of lemon-blossom, a veil of jessamine and then a cascade of frangipani, that starry flower of love and legend.

It was as if in the dim past a woman of imagination had asked that exotic blooms be planted here so that whoever came to the small palace was welcomed by untamed beauty before the walls divided widely to reveal the building itself.

Rosary leaned forward, the breath catching in her throat as the residence of the Governor came into view. It stood as if painted against the swell of the land and the arch of the sky, its stone towers and terraces as if sculptured, the iron of its curving balconies as finely filigreed as a lady's lacework. It was mellowed and perfect, as if growing from the ground itself, and there were white peacocks on its lawns, spreading their snowy fans in the golden sunlight.

She had expected Manoeline flamboyance, or a facing of *azulejos* so dear to the Portuguese heart, and instead she found grace and unforgettable charm. And as the car drew to a standstill in front of the terrace she saw the armorial crest of the family carved in the stonework above the great door. She emerged eagerly from the car, her gaze flashing from the baroque fountains to the curve of the steps leading gracefully to the columned portico.

She released her breath in a sigh of wonderment. It was a wonderful house, and she would surely be sent away as a nonentity who had no place in such an establishment!

As she stood at the foot of the steps, both entranced and struck to shyness, the front door opened and a man in neat livery came down the steps to take her suitcases and to escort her into the residence. Taking a deep breath, she preceded him, and cool upon the sunlit air was the calling of birds and the sound of water falling into the wide basins of the fountains. The peacocks strutted, certain of their place here, and their snowy beauty that enhanced the wide green lawns.

Rosary entered the hall, with a gleaming marble floor that made her feel like skimming across it. Tall smooth pillars supported an arcade in which stood marble figures and great pots of flowers. Overhead glowed a ceiling teeming with the gods and nymphs of mythology, twining and romping among suspended lamps like enormous jewels set in wrought-iron.

The coolness of purring fans made the atmosphere inviting after the warmth of the car. The manservant stood in polite silence while she studied the hall, and when she glanced at him she saw only a polite face that revealed nothing, though she knew he had been studying her. 'I will show you to your room, *senhorita*. Please to come this way.'

There were three galleries reached by a graceful wrought-iron staircase, which formed a trio of delicate iron bridges above the hall. Rosary was conducted to the upper gallery and along a corridor that was lit by sunlight through a great rose window, which sparkled as if its facets were those of a diamond. The manservant paused in front of a door and opened it, and Rosary stepped upon the firm softness of an emerald green carpet, a striking contrast to the golden wood of the furniture, and the paler gold of the long silken curtains at the balconied windows.

She had seen photographs of such rooms in stylish magazines, but never had she been ushered into one and informed it was hers; through an archway she glimpsed a smaller room and guessed it to be her private sitting-room.

Rosary just stood there, feeling as unreal as a figure in a dream. The man in livery carried her suitcases to a long stool at the foot of the big bed, draped in creamy net and covered by a green silk spread that rippled to the carpet.

A little shiver of delight ran all the way through Rosary, from the tips of her ears to her toes. This was really happening, and she was here because Cibby had insisted that she learn several languages, and Portuguese and Italian had appealed to her. When the manservant spoke to her, she understood him perfectly.

'The Senhora de Ardo will wish to speak with you.' he said. 'A message will be sent to you in a short while, when the *senhora* is free of her duties and can see you.'

'Thank you.' Rosary half-smiled at him, but with a politely blank face he withdrew from the room and quietly closed the door behind him, leaving her alone in a silence that was softly broken by the ceiling fan, which cast a wing-like shadow as it revolved. The silk curtains hung without movement at the windows, and tall flowers in a vase gave off a rather sensuous perfume.

Rosary wondered if Gisela had been lurking about to watch for her arrival, and she gazed at the door, half-hopeful that the girl would come bursting in, ready at once to be friends with her. Despite Lola's flashes of friendship during the journey, she had not at the end of it been very encouraging. Rosary troubled her lip with her teeth. She had a feeling the Senhora de Ardo was going to be rather stiff-necked and disinclined to welcome a young, modern-minded English Miss into the Governor's palace.

Restlessly she walked to a window and on impulse

13

she went out on the balcony and peered over the edge of it. The afternoon sun dazzled her eyes and her nostrils were filled with the tropical island air. It went to her head like wine and a sudden feeling of excitement raced through her blood.

Her balcony hung like a plant-basket high above a garden patio, where amid low, plant-covered walls was a large pond covered in a mass of water-lotus and their big leaves of metallic green. Further back there were willow trees, making a veil of green through which she glimpsed a lurking figure in white. She felt sure whoever it was had eyes fixed upon her balcony, seeing her there and curious. Then the veil was impenetrably green again and the white-clad figure was gone.

Someone gave a polite cough inside her room and Rosary turned and stood framed between the windows. A uniformed maid stood looking at her, and for the first time since entering the palace she was treated to an uncertain smile. She smiled back. 'Am I wanted?' she asked.

The girl nodded, and her eyes were large with surprise as they dwelt on Rosary. 'Please to come to the *sala, senhorita*. The *dona de casa* wishes to see you.'

Rosary straightened the jacket of her suit and glanced swiftly in the dressing-table mirror to make sure her hair was tidy and her nose not shiny. She saw a tense figure, chin tilted for battle. She saw that the pearl-grey suit looked good and was glad she had let Cibby buy it for her. The dusty-pink suede shoes and bag were nice, and she never wore a lot of make-up. She surely looked discreet, and if she wore a serious expression she would convince the Senhora de Ardo that she was capable.

Down the stairs they went, she and the young maid, and along a corridor lined with dark and formal portraits in carved frames. The eyes in the portraits seemed to watch her as she passed, and she thought of what Lola had said about her alien appearance. Wafted here by jet plane and car, she felt suddenly uprooted ... a daisy in a jam-jar in a place filled with porcelain pots of exotic jessamine and geranium!

The thought made her smile nervously, but was quickly suppressed as they paused in front of one of the tall doors. The maid tapped upon it, opened it, and then left Rosary to face alone the lady of the house.

'Good afternoon, Miss Bell.' The woman stood beside a window that opened on to the terrace, and there was about her an air of cool courtesy but not a hint of warmth. Her eyes saw Rosary in one swift glance, and then she came forward and indicated with a ringed hand that Rosary be seated in one of the high-backed, silk-upholstered chairs.

'Good afternoon, *senhora*.' Rosary sat down and assumed an air of composure. She was determined not to let this imperious woman undermine her confidence in her abilities. Given a fair chance she would prove that she had not wasted her own or anyone else's time in coming here. 'How delightful to see so many flowers,' she said.

'You are fond of flowers?' Senhora de Ardo bent to a table on which stood delicate teacups, a silver teapot and a cake stand on which were arranged pastries that looked almost too good to eat.

'Yes, I am a lover of gardens.' Rosary ventured a smile. 'That was one of the reasons why I wanted to come to Vozes do Mar. I had heard that it was an island of flowers.'

Rosary's smile was answered by a skimming of dark eyes that held not a glimmer of response. 'You will

15

take tea and cakes, Miss Bell?'

'I should love a cup of tea, thank you.' Rosary tried to suppress a cold little shiver; the tea, at least, would warm her chilled feelings.

'Sugar and cream?'

'Both, please.'

While the *senhora* poured the tea Rosary studied her as casually as she could. When younger her hair must have been raven dark to match her eyes, but now it was silvery and worn in a severe chignon style. There were jet pearls at her earlobes, and her dress was of dark purple silk, severely tailored, with a pattern of jet beads on the bodice. Upon both her hands were heavy-stoned rings, and one of them was a wide band of gold. A certain sternness and dignity were mingled in her features, and Rosary had the feeling that she was a widow. One of those high-born Portuguese women who were trained from girlhood to run smoothly and perfectly a household for a man, and to place romantic dreams on a lower plane to correct and rather unsmiling behaviour.

She handed Rosary her tea, and placed on the table beside her a plate, a lace-paper napkin and a silver pastry fork. 'Please to help yourself to a pastry, Miss Bell.'

'I will, *senhora*. They look delicious.'

The *senhora* nodded and sat down, as if to say that everything here at the palace had the perfect touch. Her eyes studied Rosary as she stirred her tea. 'It was understood,' she said, 'that Gisela's tutor be a person of expert knowledge. You are ... young!'

'Yes, *senhora*. But I am well trained in all that Gisela's father applied for in a tutor. My age is surely immaterial?'

'When dealing with a girl of Gisela's age and temperament discipline must be maintained. Can you be sure of doing so when you are so young yourself?'

'I can't pretend that I am a martinet,' Rosary admitted, with a slight smile. 'I happen to believe that more can be done with kindness than with severity.'

'Have you had other private pupils, Miss Bell?'

'Not private pupils, *senhora*. But as I explained in my letter to Dom Duarte I have worked as a teacher for the past year at Courland Bell's school of music in Surrey. I wished to travel, however, and when my grandfather was told by a business associate of his that the Governor of Vozes do Mar was anxious to acquire a music teacher for his daughter, I decided to apply for the post. I was trained in all I know by my grandfather, and you will, *senhora*, have heard of Irena Marcos, the Portuguese singer who is now famous in opera? She was a pupil of his, and surely there could be no better recommendation for me, that I learned at his knee and now possess knowledge I know I can pass on to Gisela.'

'You certainly sound very confident, Miss Bell.' The jetty eyes flashed over Rosary, as if assessing her clothes and her deportment. 'When my nephew decided to allow Gisela to be educated here instead of at the convent, he had in mind a post for a teacher who would stay several years on the island. I repeat that you are young, and you are attractive. You may wish to leave after a while in order to ... marry.'

'But I have no such plans,' Rosary argued. 'There is no one I have the remotest intention of marrying!'

'Really?' Senhora de Ardo arched a thin black eyebrow. 'Are British girls so different from our Latin girls? The main aim of our girls is to marry as soon as possible.'

'Aren't they married to men who are chosen for

them?' Rosary retaliated. 'If parents direct, then daughters will obey, but in my country we often choose a career in preference to domesticity, and my own grandfather would never dream of picking out a certain man for me to marry. He has taught me to think and act for myself.'

'Which may be all very well, for an English girl.' Senhora de Ardo looked all the way down her Latin nose as she said this. 'But I hope you don't intend to implant in Gisela your own rebellious ideas. Her father is a true Portuguese and naturally he has made plans for his daughter.'

Rosary didn't doubt it, but as it happened she had no intention of inciting the girl to rebel against the old and tried methods of the Portuguese of finding marital stability for their sons as well as their daughters. 'I am only interested in being a good tutor,' she replied, and she looked the *senhora* straight in the eye, letting her know that she had no intention of being cowed by her manner. 'I would not dream of imposing my personal views on Gisela. No more than I intend to have Latin views imposed on me.'

'You are outspoken, Miss Bell.'

'Yes,' said Rosary, for she didn't intend to apologize for being so. She had been hired as a tutor, not as a backstairs maid! 'I work for my living, *senhora*, but that doesn't make me a menial. If that type of person was required, then it might have been better had Dom Duarte applied outside of England. Very few of my countrywomen would tolerate these days being treated like Victorian women who had to work for a wage. I am afraid I am no Jane Eyre!'

'No.' For the briefest of moments a hint of amusement seemed to gleam in the *senhora's* eyes, then it was quickly veiled as she turned her gaze to the sunlit terrace. 'What are your views on the *palacete*? A small palace but none the less imposing, eh?'

'Quite overpowering at first glance,' Rosary agreed, a hint of humour in her own eyes. She knew what the woman meant. A girl like herself could never have lived or worked in such surroundings in her life before.

'It is a place of grace and history, Miss Bell. And many times over have the Montqueiros been in charge of the island and its people. Were my nephew a less obstinate and democratic a man he would use the title bestowed on the family many years ago.' Senhora de Ardo again met Rosary's eyes, gazing straight into them, as if to impress on her the honour it was to be in the service of her nephew. 'He is the Duque de Montqueiro, you understand, but he insists upon the lesser title of Dom Duarte.'

Despite herself Rosary was impressed ... not by the ducal title, but by the fact that this man she was yet to meet should discard what many another man would have given his eye teeth and half he owned to possess. He sounded ... intriguing.

'I hope most sincerely that Dom Duarte won't feel that my youth disqualifies me from the task which I feel mentally qualified to tackle,' she said, dabbing cream from her lips with her napkin. 'I think I should enjoy working in such superb surroundings, and not being a city girl I shan't pine for smart distractions. Gisela is allowed to swim?'

The *senhora* hesitated. 'The child, Miss Bell, is not one of your robust, hockey-playing English girls. At the age of nine she had a bad illness ...'

'At the time her mother died?' Rosary murmured.

'Exactly so. It was a great shock to the child and as there were no brothers or sisters to alleviate the loss,

Gisela took it very much to heart and she ran away...'

'Ran away?' Rosary echoed.

'Yes, in a storm. It was all terribly worrying, and when she was found she developed rheumatic fever and for several weeks we feared the worst.' The ringed hands spread themselves in a very Latin gesture. 'You will therefore understand that my nephew is extra protective of the child, and I do warn you that he will not be too pleased to find you so youthful. He will undoubtedly feel that you might not be careful enough of Gisela's health.'

'Really!' A flash of anger winged its way through Rosary. 'If she is delicate and must take care, then I shall certainly not overtax her strength in any way. I am not thoughtless, and I am certainly not flighty. If Gisela's father has laid down rules regarding his daughter, then I shall not disregard them.'

'Perhaps not,' said the *senhora*. 'But you do appear to have a lot of spirit, and it might be better if someone more placid were in charge of Gisela. Anyway, we must leave it to Duarte to decide. He is the one in authority here, and I am only in charge of the household. He will interview you. I have merely given you tea and a little advice.'

Senhora de Ardo rose to her feet, and Rosary followed her example. 'Thank you for tea and the delicious cakes,' she said. 'When will Dom Duarte wish to see me?'

'When he is free of his duties to do so,' was the dismissive reply.

'In the meantime ... could I not meet Gisela?'

'It would not be correct, Miss Bell. As I have told you, you may not be suitable and it is best that neither your hopes nor Gisela's be raised too high.'

'Then you think Gisela might like me?' Rosary

dared to say.

The woman shrugged her thin shoulders and escorted Rosary to the door of the *sala*. 'Because you are young she would immediately assume that you would let her off lessons and make of every day a holiday.' The door was opened and Rosary walked out into the hall. She felt rather like a schoolgirl, herself, being dismissed after a lecture. Lola had been right to warn her about the *dona de casa*. She wanted not a tutor of spirit about the palace, but some older and placid woman whom she could keep in her place. She wanted no sort of changes brought into these hallowed precincts by a foreign outsider, and Rosary smiled slightly as she glanced about the large hall, where everything gleamed and stood exactly in its place.

Rosary noticed a half-open door that seemed to lead out to one of the side patios, and impulsively she made for the door and stepped out into the sunlight and the scent of the flowers that softened the outlines of the enclosing walls and the scrolled iron seats.

She walked about the patio and found that one wall was covered in pomegranates, rusty-gold with their fruit. As she stood there in delight, for never before had she seen the fruits actually growing, she heard a step behind her and swung round hoping to see Gisela and to have at last a glimpse of a friendly face. Instead she was confronted by a lean young man in a dark blue shirt and brown slacks. His hair was black and rumpled, and when he slowly smiled attractive lines came into his face and his eyes admired instead of criticizing her slender figure, ashen-haired, there by the wall flamy with colourful fruit.

'Don't tell me,' he said. 'You are Persephone of the pomegranate!.'

She smiled herself, and wished he might be the Dom. Instinctively she knew him to be far too human to be a member of the Montqueiro family.

'As a matter of fact,' she said, 'I am the tutor.'

'Really?' His eyes swept over her and dwelt on her hair, which the sunshine stroked to a white-gold fairness, its thick soft curves framing her amused face. 'In my day tutors were far less attractive, all straight lines and bombazine, not to mention the silver-rimmed spectacles, and the silver in the hair. You make a most welcome addition to the palace.'

'You are kind to say so, *senhor*. But I have been warned——'

'Not about me, I hope?' He strolled closer to where she stood and with a lean hand he stroked his hair into place. He was good-looking, but not in a flaunting way, and when he stood near to her she caught a whiff of turpentine. When he introduced himself as Dacio Cortez she was not a bit surprised.

'Did you enjoy your journey here with my sister?' he asked, reaching up a hand to fondle one of the pomegranates. 'Lola likes the occasional trip to Lisbon and I expect she showed you some of the fine old buildings?'

'We did visit a couple of smart shops and a very chic restaurant,' Rosary told him drily.

He laughed, and his teeth gleamed against the dark olive of his skin. 'She is pretty, no? A lively young thing who would really like to live all the time in Lisbon, but I am her guardian and so she must live where I choose to live ... until she marries, of course.'

'Of course,' said Rosary. 'You Portuguese men seem hell-bent on believing that young women are helpless without a male shoulder to lean upon. Would you not permit Lola to take a job?'

'She has one.' He continued to smile, but a note of arrogance had crept into his voice. 'She looks after the villa and sees that I have my meals on time. Apart from that she has no need to do anything but look pretty. The nicest function in life for a girl.'

'Then you must disapprove heartily of anyone like me, who goes out to work?' Rosary gazed up at him, feeling more than ever like a girl who had stepped through a door into Victorian times. Good heavens, if this young Latin was old-fashioned with regard to women, whatever sort of man was the master of the house?

'I should be most ungallant to disapprove of someone like you.' He gave her a gallant bow to endorse his words. 'I am only sad that you have to go out alone into the world——'

'But I wanted to,' she broke in. 'I longed beyond anything else to travel and to meet people. I'd stifle tied down in a house looking after a man!'

Her words rang out, freely and defiantly, in her clear English voice, and at the same time something made her glance across the patio to where that cloistered section of it led to and from the palace. A man was standing there and he must have heard her every word. He wore an impeccable white suit with a dark tie, and there was in his bearing that indefinable air of authority that marked out each thing about him for immediate notice.

Even before he moved and came out into the sunlight, Rosary knew that he was Dom Duarte de Montqueiro Ardo.

# CHAPTER TWO

THE room in which Rosary was interviewed by Dom Duarte was a panelled study lined with books and prints. There were deep leather chairs and a large desk on lion-claw feet, its leather top much used. In a high-backed swivel chair sat the man in whose power she strangely felt now she was alone with him.

He sat there studying her in the chair facing his. His left hand toyed with a brass paperweight, and she couldn't help but notice the hands that in an earlier century would have been richly jewelled. Like their owner they had a strength and grace of movement. His hair was sable dark, growing thickly against a finely shaped head. He had the taut lines and bones of good breeding, a proud flare to his nostrils, and a rather deep groove between the blackness of his brows. She had noticed when he stood beside Dacio that he was well above the average height of the Latin male, and his eyes held a glint of steel under the oblique slant of his brows.

He was a man to notice ... a man to obey ... yet as Rosary met his eyes she was determined not to be browbeaten.

'So you are Rosary Bell, eh?' There were startling depths to his voice, and he spoke in English, the first person to address her in her own language since she had arrived here. 'You will already have spoken with the Senhora de Ardo?'

'Yes, Your Excellency.'

'There is no need to address me so formally, Miss Bell.' The glint in his eyes seemed to burn dangerously, as if he had caught the note of defiance in her voice. 'Whatever impression you made upon my aunt will not sway me one way or the other. I imagine she found you more youthful than the person we expected?'

'Yes, *senhor*. But in my opinion it might be better for Gisela to have a tutor who is not years removed from her own ideas and dreams. Your aunt told me she was a lonely child——'

'Are you lonely also, Miss Bell?' His voice seemed to have an extra resonant ring when he spoke her name, and his gaze impaled her as if upon a steel pin.

'I know what it feels like to be an only child,' she rejoined. 'I know how it can hurt never to see your mother's face again. I believe that semi-orphaned children are lonelier than other children. They are deprived of the maternal security for which material things can't compensate.'

'That is very true,' he agreed. 'But I am not in need of a mother for Gisela, merely a competent person who will stimulate her interest in music and make of her an interesting young woman.'

Rosary flushed, for it seemed to her heightened senses that he implied that she was here in order to interest *him*. She felt like telling him that in the first place she had not known of his eligibility; and in the second place he was not in any way the type of man she could fall in love with. He was imperious beyond belief, and certainly he had no need to use his ducal title when his entire manner was so cool and haughty.

'By letter you approved my qualifications for this post,' she said, in her coolest voice. 'And it would be unfair to send me away before I have proved or disproved my competency as a tutor.'

'I quite agree,' he said. 'Despite your youth, I am

going to allow you to stay a while on approval.'

'Approval!' she exclaimed. 'Like a washing machine? No, thank you!' She rose to her feet and her eyes were stormy. Not only was she the granddaughter of Courland Bell, she was one of his star graduates, and she'd be darned if this Portuguese duke would speak to her as if he were taking on trial a gauche parlourmaid. 'I think, *senhor*, that it would be better if you found someone more staid and therefore, in your opinion, more suitable——'

'Sit down,' he ordered. 'Instantly.'

She stared at him, and then once again she flushed. He made her feel as if she had behaved like a school-girl.

'You are not in the least like a washing machine,' he crisped. 'You are more like a young cat on edge in a strange house. Sit down, Miss Bell, and stop glaring at me.'

She hesitated, hating herself for being a little afraid of him. She sat down, stiffly, a slim and offended figure in the high-backed chair of dark carving that pressed against her bones. It was an inquisitorial chair, like the eyes that studied her, taking in with a cool object-ivity her fair English looks in this sombre panelled room ... the only room she had so far seen which was not fragrant with vases of island flowers.

'Have you ever worked privately before, *senhorita*?'

'No,' she admitted. 'I have been a teacher at the school, but if I work here, it will be my first private tutorial.'

'You have seen something of the *palacete*. Do you think it would suit you to work here?'

'Without a doubt, *senhor*. I—I sense its history, its appeal to the imagination. As I explained to your aunt, it appealed greatly to me to journey abroad to work.'

'Your grandfather made no objection?'

'On the contrary. He thought it would broaden my mind, and my appreciation of music, to meet people of a culture so different from my own. Even as I teach Gisela, I shall be studying your Portuguese folk music and melodies.'

'Have you no ambition to be a concert pianist, Miss Bell?'

She thought over his words, and for the first time in his presence she gave a slight smile. 'It would be marvellous to follow into the concert world my parents, who were a dual team. My mother played as my father's accompanist. He was a superb violinist. I can't remember him so well as I remember my mother, for he was always practising and shut away from a child's noise. But I have albums of his recordings and I know how fine a musician he was. I believe my mother could have been a soloist had she chosen to be, but I am told by Courland Bell that she sacrificed her solo triumphs for the sake of ... love.'

The steely Latin eyes dwelt thoughtfully on Rosary's uplifted face, then he arose to his feet and approached a smoking table on which stood a carved box and a swan-shaped lighter. He opened the box and took from it a small cigar. He clipped the end and placed it in the flame, then he carried the cigar to his lips. Rosary's eyes followed the movement, and for the first time she noticed that his mouth was more sensuous than the rest of his firmly chiselled features.

It was faintly disturbing and made her wonder why he had never remarried. Had he loved his wife too well ever to bother again with marriage?

'So you desired to travel?' he said. 'You are not the

type for being tied to domesticity?'

She knew he had caught the words which she had flung at Dacio, and through the cigar smoke she saw a gleam of amusement in his eyes, as if he thought her young and impetuous.

'What is wrong, *senhor*, in wanting a career? The women of your own country are beginning to clamour for more freedom, and I don't blame them.'

'I am sure you don't. However, most women find it temperamentally more suitable, and perhaps even more exciting, to let themselves be loved and married.'

'Men certainly find it more suitable,' she retorted, 'to have someone always on hand to wait on them, flatter them and be blamed if anything upsets them.'

He was silent when she finished speaking and he just stood looking at her, his cigar smoke wreathing about his lips, his high cheekbones, and his rather imperious nose. It was a look that said she was foolish and untouched by the emotions that drove a woman into the arms of a man; it was a look which reminded her that he no longer had a wife for his consolation, or his martyr.

'From a moralistic point of view you will be perfect for Gisela,' he said, smoothly drawling the words. 'There seems no doubt that you have spent most of your time in study. But all the same I am going to insist that you are engaged as tutor for a trial run of six weeks. My aunt no doubt told you that I wish Gisela to be tutored for several years, but I must be certain that she is in the charge of the best possible teacher. As a parent I am not being unreasonable, and you accept my terms, Miss Bell, or you leave tomorrow. It is for you to decide.'

'The decision seems to be yours, *senhor*,' she replied. 'It seems I must agree to your terms or return home like—like an expelled schoolgirl.'

'Then you agree to remain on approval?' His lip twitched as he spoke.

'I have no choice but to agree, *senhor*. The island appeals to me, and I am obstinate. I like to prove myself.'

'Six weeks should give you ample time in which to prove your worth, *senhorita*. As my daughter's tutor and companion you will take your meals at my table. You will set aside the cooler hours for walking, riding and playing games. In the heat of the afternoon I shall require Gisela to take *siesta*. She is not entirely robust, though I am assured by our doctor that sensible exercise can do her no harm. Sometimes I may wish myself and certain of my guests to be entertained by your musical ability as a pianist, Miss Bell. I hope you will agree to play for us. There is a fine grand piano in the music *sala*, and another smaller instrument has been provided for the use of Gisela. Now, have you any questions?'

'I shall be free to make a few friends of my own, *senhor*?'

'But of course, so long as you confine your friendships to people known to me. While you are here you will be my responsibility, and even on a Portuguese island it is not unknown for a young girl to go astray.'

'You mean in the company of a young man?' she said drily.

'Exactly so.'

'But I am the studious, not the flirtatious type, Dom Duarte.'

'As a Portuguese I know my countrymen, *senhorita*. Quite frankly I did wish for a sober-looking, more mature woman to be in charge of Gisela. You are neither of those things, and therefore you will be a source of interest to the young men of Vozes do Mar. Surely I am not incorrect in saying that Dacio Cortez has already flattered you?'

For a fighting instant Rosary felt inclined to tell this dominant male creature that in her free time she would please herself, and make her own friends, and be flattered by them if she wished, but upon meeting his eyes she decided that discretion was the better part of valour. He wouldn't hesitate to send her packing if she defied the rules laid down for her correct behaviour. Not only was he Portuguese but he was of the ancient, ruling order who would not release too readily their hold on the restrictive chains attached to the females in their care. It was a protective attitude, but it also ensured that the man remained the master.

'You were about to say?' He quirked an eyebrow in mocking politeness.

'That I must not be too exuberant in my—attachments, is that correct, *senhor*?'

'I should not advise it.'

'But as you requested Senhorita Cortez to meet me in Lisbon, you can surely have no objection to a friendship between myself and the Cortez couple?'

'They live within the precincts of the *palacete*, therefore you are bound to have contact with them. I merely ask you not to be seen alone with strangers.'

'*I* am a stranger, *senhor*. I am English and I have ways different from your own women.'

'Naturally. And that is why I suggest that you moderate them to match the discretion expected by the Portuguese of young women. This is a Portuguese island and your looks will seem alien enough to those who have not travelled in other parts of the world. You comprehend?'

'I am to behave demurely,' she replied. 'To stand by

the rules, and to be available as an entertainer when you have guests.'

An instant and dangerous silence followed her words, and she almost felt those steely fingers hustling her off the hallowed soil of Vozes do Mar. Then he gave a shrug and seemed to dismiss her remark as the sort he would soon tame on her tongue.

'Then it is agreed that you stay,' he said. 'I shall write to explain the terms to your grandfather, and to assure him that I shall see you come to no harm.'

'Very well, *senhor*.' She suppressed a quick smile, picturing Cibby's amusement when he realized that she would be working for the type of man her independence would strike against like flint against steel. He would chuckle, that grand old man of humour and forbearance. He would know that Dom Duarte de Montqueiro Ardo had admitted a spirited young cat into his dovecote, and that a few feathers were bound to fly in the coming weeks.

She stood up, for instinct told her that the interview was at an end. She followed him as he strode to the door and opened it. For a moment as she stood quite near to him she realized his height, his authority and a certain iron charm to the smile he slanted down at her. 'I am sure we shall come to an understanding of each other before too long, Miss Bell. In the meantime avail yourself of the music room, the library and the gardens. You are sure to find Gisela in one of them and the two of you must make friends. If at any time you wish to discuss a problem with me, then you have only to seek me out. I am not entirely the stern and hidebound tyrant, you know.'

She accepted this remark in silence and wondered if she was expected to give him a curtsey on making her departure from his ducal presence. As she looked at him a subtle change came over his face and he seemed to read her mind with alarming speed.

'I see that you have formed an opinion of me, Miss Bell. You have decided that I am still at the turn of the century in my ideas, and that I rule my daughter, my household and this island with the inflexible hand in the velvet gauntlet. *Por Deus*, you English have a cool arrogance of your own which would be hard to match! You make your way through the world believing that everything should be as the English think best. Well, *senhorita*, my daughter is a Portuguese girl and you have not been hired to fill her head with some of your own foolish notions ... those regarding men and women in particular. I happen still to believe that women are ruled by their emotions, and if we placed this world in their hands it would soon become a crazy Disneyland filled with gingerbread castles and fashion parlours!'

'And what is wrong with that, *senhor*?' Rosary asked demurely. 'Surely it would be better than making war?'

'You imagine that women make no sort of war?' His eyes and his voice took on a dangerous, velvety smoothness.

'Of course they don't! Women hate war!'

'Then how young you really are!' He smiled and showed the gleaming edge of his teeth. 'They make a battlefield of each meeting with a man. They arm themselves for battle in silk and perfume, and they use the most deadly of weapons ... seduction.'

And so saying he clicked his heels, bowed and withdrew into his study. The door closed, leaving her alone in the wide marbled hall, where the fans purred and wafted to her the scent of flowers. Go to the library or the music room, he had said, but he had given her no directions, and there seemed no one around whom she could ask. She glanced at her wristwatch and saw that the afternoon was waning. She would go to her room instead and unpack her belongings, and take another look at the quarters she would occupy for the next few weeks.

As she walked up the marble stairs with the scrolled iron balustrade she tried to remember the exact location of her apartment. Although called a small palace, it seemed immense to her, with the columns rearing high to hold the three galleries with their various rooms and arcades; their corridors and odd little flights of steps leading, she imagined, to belvederes.

She paused on the second gallery and glanced about for the gemmed lighting of the rose window. Ah, there it was! And the tall door of her apartment was on the left. She turned the wrought-brass handle and entered, and after closing the door behind her she kicked off her shoes and walked about in her nyloned feet on the thick velvet carpet while she unpacked her cases and hung in the deep closet her dresses and skirts, her tailored trouser-suit and her two evening gowns. She had wondered if she should pack them, and as she stroked the chiffon and the silk, she thought of her employer's remark that he would wish her upon occasion to play for himself or his guests.

She placed her lingerie in the long drawer at the foot of the dress closet, and she smiled, ruefully, at her own image of him during the air journey from London and the boat trip from Lisbon. Portuguese men had seemed to her more stocky than tall, and good-looking in the usual dark-haired, olive-skinned fashion of the Latin male. She had thought of him with a wife to whom he was devoted. She had believed he would be benevolent, and not entirely interested in the pursuits of his girl child.

How different was the reality from that Dom Duarte she had imagined!

She opened a door leading out of her sitting-room, and caught her breath first in amazement, and then in delight. It was a bathroom and the walls were tiled with *azulejos*, some in patterns and others to represent mermaids, sea-horses, boats and giant shells. It was a mad and wonderful bathroom, with a tub sunk into the floor, a shower fixed overhead and a pale blue lavatory and bidet set side by side. It was foreign, and luxurious, and irresistibly inviting to Rosary who had been travelling since the early hours and craved a soak in bubbly, scented water.

She set about filling the deep tub with water, and added her own bubble-bath lotion, though there were glass shelves of various bath aids with expensive labels on them. She placed fresh lingerie on the padded stool, and then she stood indecisive and wondered if the family dressed formally for dinner. She tried to imagine Dom Duarte looking informal and found that her imagination wouldn't stretch that far. He was the type of autocrat who only bent his straight backbone in a brief courteous bow, and was never anything but impeccable in appearance and aloof in behaviour. She couldn't picture him with a hair out of place ... nor with the wild urges of passion storming through his veins. She couldn't help but wonder if Gisela was the result of an arranged marriage.

Then, with a shrug, Rosary took from her bedroom closet a dress of pale shantung, simply cut, but with wrist-length sleeves of nude silk, the wristbands embroidered with silver roses. She studied it with a wicked little gleam in her eyes and decided to wear it. It might not be as formal as his lordship would wish, but it had a long skirt and he obviously wished that women were still hampered by the bustle and the train!

She laid the dress across the foot of her bed and went to have her bath. The water was warm and delicious and she lay in a veil of bubbles and drowsed with her head against the rubber headrest. Never in her wildest dreams had she ever imagined herself as a tutor in a palace of all places! Yet here she was, luxuriating in a scented bath and lulled by the low, persistent chorus of the cicadas as evening began to fall and the sun's strength died in the hot-cold flame of sunset.

There was beauty here on this island called Voices of the Sea. The name itself was like music ... and there her thoughts broke off as the door of the bathroom was suddenly pushed open and a figure appeared in the doorway. Rosary's eyes flew open in alarm, and she seemed half-mermaid herself as she lay there half concealed by bubbles, her fair hair pinned to the crown of her head, with wet tendrils clinging to her neck.

She and the invader of her privacy stared at each other. 'You are Gisela!' she exclaimed, even as the girl said: 'You are Miss Bell!'

They laughed together, and then gravity masked the young face once again. It was a thin face, with high cheekbones, an oval chin and very dark eyebrows. It might have been a plain face but for the oblique dark eyes set round with dense short lashes. It was, in fact, a rather oriental face, Rosary thought, and as this girl grew older and developed poise, those eyes would make of her quite an enchantress.

'I hoped we would meet today,' smiled Rosary, 'but I hoped with a little more dignity on my part.'

'It was Dacio who suggested I introduce myself. He

35

said I should be surprised by you.'

'I know! Like your father you expected a martinet with a rule book in her hand and a bun on her head. Instead you find me without a stitch on my person.'

'I had better go into the other room while you dress——'

'Don't run away,' said Rosary. 'Stay there and we will have a little talk.'

'*Sim, senhorita.*' Gisela withdrew into the bedroom and closed the mirrored door behind her. Rosary released the bath water and stood up to let the cool shower water rinse the soap bubbles from her body. In the mirrored panels she could see herself, slender and pale-skinned, with long, slim and rather pretty legs. Although it was true that she had been wrapped up in her musical and linguistic studies for the past few years, there had been young students at the school who had wished to become closer acquainted with her. In particular there had been Erick Stornheim, an Austrian composer rather older than the students; a friend of Cibby's, who had sent her several expensive gifts, Swiss chocolates, French gloves and web-fine stockings.

As she swathed her body in a large soft towel, she remembered that last time she had seen him, in the drawing-room of Cibby's house. The lazy, smouldering look in his penetrating blue eyes, when she had walked in from her classes, books under her arm, her fair hair swinging and her skirt a short one. Without asking permission he had reached out a hand to touch her hair, blown in the wind as she crossed the lawns of the adjacent school building. His hand had slipped to the soft wool of her sweater.

'You grow lovely, *liebchen*,' he had said. 'It seems but yesterday when first I saw you as a *real* schoolgirl.'

Rosary turned away from her reflection as she

slipped into her lingerie, and she wondered briefly about men and their passions. The secret side of male hunger was still unknown to her, and at times it half scared her. As the brief silky garments covered her slim and untouched body, and she felt the smoothness of her own skin, the firm delicacy of her structure, she knew with certainty that she would have to be madly in love with a man before she ever gave herself.

She wasn't old-fashioned, but she felt rather sad for girls who thought it fun to experiment with all that secret side of life ... which could surely only offer the ultimate with a man adored?

She tied the belt of her robe and entered the bedroom, where Gisela stood by the balcony doors and watched the darkening of the sky. The girl turned as she heard Rosary, and her smile was hesitant. 'Is my father going to permit you to stay?' she asked.

'Don't you wish me to stay?' Rosary countered, taking the pins from her hair and brushing it into a long, almost straight swathe about her shoulders. She looked young, and she felt far more unsure than she liked to admit. It was essential that she and Gisela like each other, for it seemed certain that the Senhora de Ardo was not going to unbend very easily, and Rosary didn't even try to imagine Dom Duarte on amicable terms with her. That man was a creature of steel sheathed in dark velvet! No doubt he had charm, of a remote kind, which he rationed out to those of whom he approved.

Rosary had answered him back and defended her right to have a mind and a will of her own.

'The only wishes that count are my father's,' said Gisela.

'But he allowed you home from the convent, he said you might have a private tutor. Are you disappointed

37

in me, Gisela?'

'It is too early to say.' The girl stared at Rosary's fair hair, which seemed unreal in contrast to her eyes. Rosary had always thought of them as brown until the evening Cibby had poured brandy for himself and Erick Stornheim. The Austrian had raised his glass and said deliberately that her eyes were the colour of cognac ... and indeed they were. A deep golden brown, not only the colour of cognac, but with a warmth, a slumbering fire and tiny sparks of gaiety.

'Is your hair really that colour?' Gisela asked, with the frankness of youth. 'One of our teachers at the convent used to dye her hair black.'

'I can assure you mine doesn't come out of a bottle.' Rosary walked out on to the balcony and breathed the air, which seemed even more intoxicating now that darkness lay over the island and the glimmer of golden star-points could be seen. 'Jessamine,' she murmured. 'Perfume of the Arabian Nights. No wonder you couldn't stay away, Gisela. You must love this island.'

'I was born here, and so was my mother, and her mother. I am a true islander, Miss Bell. Way back in my mother's family there is Arabian blood, for there was a time when the island was occupied by them. Some of the girls were put into *harems*, and then they were rescued when the Portuguese took the island back again.' Gisela breathed an excited little sigh as she stood upon the curved balcony with Rosary. 'I do think everything was terribly exciting in those olden days. There were armoured knights and pirates. Arabian lords and girls who were veiled all the way down from their eyes!'

Rosary smiled. 'When we start our lessons we will read all the old operas and ballets together. I am sure you will love them.'

'Then my father has asked you to stay?'

'He has given me a trial term of six weeks. I am to prove in that time that I am a good teacher, and if I don't satisfy his requirements I shall be dismissed.'

Gisela stood quiet a moment, stroking a pale blossom that sprouted through the ironwork of the balcony enclosure. It was almost a *miradoura* from the days when women had watched in terror the approach of pirate galleons. Rosary half-closed her eyes as a soft and sensuous breeze stirred her loosened hair and the wide sleeves of her robe. How almost easy to imagine this island as untouched by the modern world, governed as it was by a feudal aristocrat who even in a tailored white suit gave the impression of being clad in armour.

'Did my father make you feel nervous?' Gisela asked, a knowing note in her voice.

'Of course not,' said Rosary, a little too quickly. 'We merely discussed your lessons, the recreations we shall enjoy together, and the time when you take siesta. I am sure that if we get along smoothly there will be no need for your father to disapprove. The root of all learning is that the student and the tutor should be compatible. The parent should not interfere, even if the teacher is not to his personal liking.'

'Did my father seem not to like you, Miss Bell?'

'The feeling was mutual——' Rosary bit her lip, for this was hardly a remark to make to his teenage daughter. 'Perhaps, Gisela, you would like to call me by my first name? It would be more friendly, and less likely to make me feel the Victorian governess.'

'I don't know your first name——'

'It's Rosary.'

'You mean like prayer beads?' Gisela gave a small excited gasp.

39

'If you like, Gisela. But the name also means a rose arbour.'

'How romantic to have so unusual a name!'

'I think Gisela is rather fable-like. There is a ballet called *Giselle*, and what could be more romantic than that?'

Gisela shrugged and wandered back into the bedroom, where she stood by the fourposter and stroked the long skirt of the dress that lay across the bed. 'Aunt Azinha will expect you to be drab and retiring,' she said. 'She won't like it if you look too glamorous. She will think you are setting your cap at my father.'

'What an idea!' Rosary frowned at the dress and wondered after all if it would be better if she wore something more subdued.

'It isn't that Aunt Azinha would object to him marrying again,' Gisela continued, 'but she would naturally expect him to marry a Portuguese woman of his own class.'

Rosary gave the girl an amused look. 'Even if I were a duchess, my dear, I would still not be your father's type, or he mine. I was not brought up to treat any man like a god, but I am aware that the Latin attitude to marriage is different from ours. Here the man is the master, but in my country the partners are equal, and the woman speaks her mind when it pleases her.'

Rosary picked up the silk dress and with a pang of regret she hung it away in the closet and took out instead a simple brown dress with a white, appliquéd collar. She saw ahead of her some inevitable clashes with Dom Duarte, but she wished to stay on the right side of Senhora de Ardo. In any household it was more comfortable all round if the mistress was a friend and not an enemy.

'Do you think this dress is more suitable?' she asked

Gisela, with a slight smile. 'This is my first post in a Portuguese household and I don't wish to do the wrong thing.'

'Such a dress will make you look more subdued,' Gisela agreed. 'Does it feel very strange to be living here—Rosary?'

'Strange, but interesting, and I'm looking forward to exploring the island with your help. I'm sure it's very lovely, and I want to soak up all the sunshine I can, as well as the history and legends, and the folk music. I want to know the island and its people, and not feel too much the stranger.' Rosary stood thoughtful a moment, holding the brown dress that would make her seem more like a governess in the eyes of her employer and his aunt. 'I suppose I want to feel—accepted.'

'Which means you will have to conform.' Gisela's rather serious young face took on an impish look. 'Portuguese people make a lot of rules for young women to obey.'

'Such as?' Rosary sat down in a cane chair and prepared to listen; her eyes were amused, but she knew that up to a point she must conform if she was to become part of the island community. She would remain alien to these people if she shrugged off their rules of etiquette as old-fashioned.

'The foremost rule for girls is that male friends are taboo, and only the young man selected for one's future husband is permitted to call, or to take one for a car ride, or to the theatre. And even when alone the couple are on their honour to behave discreetly. Often a father insists that they be chaperoned by an aunt or a cousin, in case their feelings for each other should become too warm. Then,' Gisela added, 'when they are married, the husband is dominant, and the wife is

41

often obliged to live in the household of her mother-in-law.'

'How delightful,' Rosary murmured. 'Your men may be handsome, Gisela, but I shall make an effort not to fall in love with one of them.'

'But love happens, whether we want it or not,' Gisela said, with the reasonable, and surprising precociousness of the Latin schoolgirl.

'Falling in love could prove awkward for a Portuguese couple, when marriages are arranged by the parents,' said Rosary. 'How do you convent girls skate around that little problem?'

Gisela gave a little laugh. 'Many Portuguese girls fall in love with the young man chosen for them.'

'The wish being father to the thought, eh? If you must marry the man, then you might as well love him?'

'Portuguese girls are practical,' Gisela agreed. 'It is often the men who are idealistic. They have a saying: Illusion is a great enchantress—she attracts and seduces.'

'Illusion, mother of romance,' Rosary murmured, thoughtful eyes upon the girl who lounged against a carved post of the enormous bed, young in body and yet old in the head, with deep in her blood the sophistication of the east. 'Exactly how old are you, Gisela?'

'I am almost fifteen. Sometimes on this island girls are married at the age of fifteen.'

Rosary was not shocked. She knew that all things tropical came to an early blooming, that for a few years they were lovely as tropical flowers, and then as that ripe bloom faded they grew plump and languid and were immersed in raising several children. To an English girl it was a little sad rather than shocking, but it was the custom, the way of life, and no doubt practical for a hot-natured people.

'I don't think, Gisela, that your father plans to marry you off so young,' she said. 'And now I had better get dressed for dinner! Do you join us at late table?'

'Yes. And then I am allowed half an hour in the *sala* before going to bed.' Gisela smiled. 'I am already treated as quite grown up. My father is a worldly man.'

'You will be company for me!' Rosary had been anticipating with reluctance the evening that lay ahead in the company of Dom Duarte and his rather severe aunt. 'I am pleased!'

Gisela gazed at her, and her cheekbones flushed. 'You are different from Lola,' she said. 'Lola likes to be alone with my father.'

Rosary was not surprised. She had somehow formed the opinion herself that the vivacious Portuguese girl had a crush on the Governor of the island. She had spoken hopefully of hearing that Rosary was unsuitable for the post of tutor ... by now her brother Dacio would have told her that the English girl was staying.

# CHAPTER THREE

THIS was the second week Rosary had spent at the *palacete*, and each morning she never failed to feel wonderment when she awoke to find sunlight bright against the walls of her room, and sprawled like a golden cloak across her bed. Breakfast would be brought to her by a young maid, and because she couldn't get enough of the sunshine, so rationed at home by the English climate, she would eat on her balcony and feel the touch of the sun on her white skin. She wanted so much to become tanned. She felt so conspicuous when she took walks with Gisela and people stared at her hair and her pallor in contrast to their sun-browned vigour.

She loved the fact that her balcony overlooked that old part of the garden, where the lotus flowers spun on the dark green skirts of their leaves, and where in the night a thousand frogs made it their park. In the distance, the far blue distance, lay the mountains of colder lands, but here on Vozes do Mar it seemed eternal summer, and she knew with each new day that she had wanted all her life to find a place where the beauty of nature was unspoiled by noise and smoke of traffic; great tall buildings, and people always in a hurry.

Here the life had a slower beat, a warm and sensuous quality, with the island gone to a golden stillness in the afternoon hours, when shutters were closed against the blaze of the sun and the wives and workers took their siesta.

Clad in a brown shirt and a crisp white blouse,

Rosary ate rolls with quince jam, and drank a second cup of tea. It seemed that the *senhora* was fond of tea and it was an available blessing for someone English, like Rosary, who preferred coffee at lunchtime. A slim silver bracelet shone on her wrist, and her hair was clipped back softly at the nape of her neck. She knew that she was expected to look efficient and she did her best to look the part. It was during the siesta, when Gisela rested, that Rosary let loose her hair and her feelings on the beach that shelved from the terraced gardens of the palace. There she swam and explored the rocky coves and groynes. There she made sketches and notes, and ran about in bare feet.

If the Dom knew that she spent the siesta in this way, he never spoke of it. If he disapproved, it was just too bad. She needed during the day a break from routine, and after a morning of lessons Gisela was always ready for a rest in her cool, shuttered room.

Her breakfast completed, Rosary left her apartment and walked along the quiet corridor to the stairs. A study at the far end of the hall had been provided for the lessons; a small rotunda in which the piano stood between the windows, with a wide padded bench, and a table piled with folios of music. Gisela's mother had been a friend of Irena Marcos, the singer, so there had always been music available for her whenever she came on a visit.

She still came, Gisela said, and she was every bit as lovely as her rich soprano voice. Rosary half remembered her, for Cibby had been her teacher. She had seemed a dark-haired goddess, who smiled distantly at young things in gym-slips. Now, if they met again, it would be as women assessing each other's attraction with regard to the opposite sex.

Rosary opened the door of the study, but Gisela was

not yet down. It was still quite early, and a stroll outdoors would be pleasant while she awaited her pupil.

She wandered along the crazy-paved paths where gardeners were already at work among the lawns and the bright beds of flowers. Gay green birds flew about, and the silvery stalks of asphodel brushed her legs as she walked around a curving wall of the palace and smelled the white lavender massed beneath a window. Suddenly she halted and drew back into the shadow of a ferny tree as a figure in light grey suiting came out upon the front steps. He stood a moment, there between the marble columns, then he turned his dark head and looked directly at Rosary.

'Good morning, Miss Bell.' He inclined his head, and his gaze was so insistent that it drew her out from among the fronds of greenery. 'I see you are up early as usual. Your energy is confounding, but don't overdo things until you are more used to our climate.'

She knew at once that he was referring to the fact that she never took a siesta, and as always with this man she felt the urge to offer a little defiance. 'I'm so interested in everything, *senhor*, that I don't get tired.'

'Excellent. I am pleased that we don't bore you.' He stood there with great assurance, and he carried his shoulders as if they wore a cloak, the full and sweeping *cambiada*. Somehow he had the features and the attributes of a man of bygone days, and even the modern tailoring of his suit, the narrow cut of the lapels and the trousers, and the hip vents of the jacket could not dispel that air he had of ancient nobility and proud instincts.

Rosary felt the flick of his eyes over her slim sedateness, and for a startled moment she wondered if he had seen her in her bathing suit on the beach, with her hair in damp disorder. He was always so impeccable himself that an untidy woman would seem, she felt sure, distasteful to him.

'I hope you find my daughter a good pupil?' he said. 'I must say that she seems of a less serious countenance these days. My aunt informs me that she often hears the two of you laughing together.'

'Yes, *senhor*. But we don't waste time. We are reading the plays of Molière, and you will admit——'

'Quite.' He held up a lean, restraining hand, and a glint of amusement came and went in his eyes. 'Molière is amusing, and very worldly. I must get used to the idea that I have acquired for my daughter a tutor of exceptional intelligence.'

'Thank you, *senhor*.' She spoke stiffly, for she felt sure he was being a little mocking. He was a Latin and such men did not admire intellectual qualities in a woman. 'It isn't that I am trying to impose my tastes upon Gisela, but I am pleased to say that she enjoys reading the plays. She is very grown up for her years——'

'So I am aware, Miss Bell. Ah, here is my car, and I will bid you *adeus*.'

He went down the steps with a lithe ease of body, and took the wheel of the streamlined Porsche, a car which somehow suited the *grande* elegance of the man. It did, she thought, in place of a mettlesome horse with a high saddle. It suited today the way he was dressed, but she had not yet seen him on horseback and had an idea she would like to ... for the sake of artistic appeal.

He drove off, swiftly and with assurance, and Rosary entered the palace and as the coolness of the purring fans struck at her face and neck, she realized that her cheeks were hot. She stood there in the hall, hands to her cheeks, and was unaware for several seconds that a male figure was lounging against the balustrade of the stairs and was regarding her with amused interest.

'You look, *senhorita*, less serene than usual,' drawled Dacio. 'Has our eminent Governor been rebuking you ... or paying you a compliment?'

Rosary glanced up and her eyes were startled because her thoughts had been so occupied by the man who had just driven away; her eyes against the pale frame of her hair were a deep gold-brown, an illusion of velvet flowers, which Dacio seemed to reach forward to pluck as she looked at him.

'Dom Duarte has an unpredictable quality,' she said. 'Without moving a muscle he gives one the feeling that he might pounce.'

'To kiss, or strike?'

'No—to the first!' she said hastily. 'I shouldn't care to make an enemy of the *duque*. Even as a friend he might prove uncome-atable.'

'As opposed to uncomfortable?'

'Yes. I can see he has charm, of an aloof sort. But I don't envy those women who—love him.'

'Frightening, eh?'

'Terribly fastidious! Dacio, did you know Gisela's mother?'

The artist shook his black hair, which grew rather long and was attractively untidy. He took the three steps that brought him to her side. 'Come with me and I will show you her portrait.'

Rosary hesitated, and Dacio took her by the hand and drew her to the stairs. 'It won't take but a few minutes, and curiosity will buzz in your brain until it is satisfied.'

'Was she beautiful?' Rosary walked with him up the curving staircase and she felt a mounting sense of excitement. It would surely give her a clue to the inner man to see the face of the woman who had actually shared his life. 'You as an artist must know beauty when you see it?'

'There are varying kinds, *senhorita*. Many lines and curves and fleeting moments that create beauty. It can't always be captured, that look, that turn of the head, that fleeting smile, and only the sun is the perfect artist, and sometimes the sun is cruel and reveals what a little dusk might turn to loveliness.'

'You speak like a poet, Dacio.'

'A touch of poety is not out of place in a painter.' He flashed a smile at her, and an answering smile lit her eyes. When they paused on the bend of the second gallery she waited for him to lead her to the portrait of the woman who had once been the mistress of this marvellous house ... someone who must have been reared for such a position, such a man as Dom Duarte.

Dacio beckoned her through an archway, and at last she was seeing the picture gallery, a panorama of small, large and enormous paintings, stretching along the walls to the turn of the room, created by artists of varying degrees of talent, and most of them in fine old frames of gilt or carved wood. Some of them were landscapes, a captured gem of a house set among trees, or a baroque church among quaint cottages. The walls were alive with their movement and their colour, but here and there were blank spaces and upon a large table at the centre of the gallery were paintings which had been removed from their frames and were undergoing removal of stain and bloom, and the restoration of rich or pastel colouring.

'Oh—it would take hours, days to enjoy all these!' Rosary gazed about her with delight. 'How many, many years it must have taken for so large a collection to crowd these walls!'

She glanced upwards and saw a ceiling of turquoise glass, a long arching dome that poured a sort of sea-light down into the gallery.

'Some of the paintings are not so good,' said Dacio, 'but there are others worth a lot of money. Dom Duarte has an eye for real art, so I am here to restore part of the collection, and the remainder will be crated and stored away in the vaults. He has decided that the gallery will be much improved as a show place if the more worthwhile pictures are better arranged so as ot reveal their individual beauty or distinction.'

'Yes,' she agreed, and then she gave a little laugh. 'But some of the fun of hunting for a treasure will be lost. Now, Dacio, do show me the wife he loved!'

Dacio raised a slow and taunting eyebrow as he stood there looking at her, with the sea-blue light sheening her hair, mystifying her eyes, softening the crisp whiteness of her blouse and blue-shading her slim white neck.

'How romantic you sound, *senhorita*. Do you believe that a man and a woman marry only from love?'

'As an English person I like to believe it,' she said, her gazed fixed upon a flower study that had the charm of a bygone, more romantic age. 'I do know, of course, that the arranged marriage is still a part of Portuguese life. Are you saying, Dacio, that the *senhor's* marriage was one of expediency rather than love?'

'Come and judge for yourself.' He took her lightly by the wrist and led her to the table where he had some canvases at rest against a chair. He cleared a space on the table and lifted one of the canvases to the flat surface. The light caught the brushwork, the texture of the deep red velvet of the dress, with a full skirt just showing the velvet slippers decorated by silk pearl-coloured roses. Rosary's gaze moved slowly upwards, taking in the plump hands clasped in the rich velvet and weighted with rings. Her gaze followed the swan-like neck as it arose from the V of the dress and she stared at the vivid, oval face with that touch of the orient in the dark slanting eyes and the glossy pile of dark hair.

'Isabela de Montquiero Ardo.' Dacio spoke the name with a sort of reluctant admiration. 'She was beautiful, of course, but too – too exotic for my taste.'

'Superb,' Rosary murmured, but with a sense of shock she was thinking to herself. 'Isabela was stunning, but like an orchid that might hate to be handled!'

'Look at that ruby necklace,' Dacio murmured. 'She knew how well that rich colour suited the rich texture of her skin. Strange. She should strike a man as sensuous, and yet I merely have the feeling that she was really as cool as marble.'

'Then,' said Rosary, 'they must have been a well-suited couple.'

'Does *he* strike you that way?' Dacio slanted a look at Rosary. 'He's self-contained, but even a volcano has been known to bear ice.'

'You know him better than I.' Rosary smiled with a touch of devilry, and leaned forward to study the beauty of Isabela's face. That marriage had been no mating of a demure dove and an arrogant duke ... each had wanted something from the other. A desire, brilliant in the eyes of the woman, for jewels and splendid gowns. A wish on the part of the man for a son, perhaps. But instead Gisela had been born and after her birth there had been no more children.

'How did she die?' Rosary couldn't help but think it

cruel that so beautiful a woman should have died so comparatively young.

'Her death was a dramatic one.' Dacio glanced along the gallery to the entrance and his voice sank down, as if he didn't wish to be overheard. 'Gisela may not know the full facts ... one cannot tell, for she's an oddly adult young creature, with a touch of secretiveness. It was an accident, you see, which killed Isabela. Dom Duarte liked to ride and sometimes she would go with him, clad in one of those dashing, full-skirted riding-habits which make it necessary for a woman to ride side-saddle. They had gone off together in an amicable mood, but when they returned Isabela was riding like a fury and whipping her horse until the poor creature leapt and bounded in an attempt to escape the lash. It was a thoroughbred, sable-black, and unused to being treated like a mule. As he came bounding into the stableyard, he suddenly reared up where the stone arches and Isabela struck her head, lost control of the animal and was dragged beneath the stamping hooves. Dom Duarte threw himself out of his own saddle and ran to catch the reins of the black horse ... his wife in her purple habit was there under the hooves, and there was blood all over her face. She had been kicked above the left temple and half her cheek had been laid open. She breathed for ten minutes, but by the time the doctor arrived she was dead.'

In the silence which followed Dacio's account of the tragic accident, Rosary could almost hear her heart beating. How terrible! And how Dom Duarte must blame himself for having quarrelled with her! And how shocking must have been the quarrel to have roused her to such a temper, which she had taken out on the poor brute of a horse.

A slow, cold shudder ran through Rosary, for Dacio,

with his eye for dramatic detail, had painted a too vivid picture of the tragedy.

'I hope Gisela doesn't know the full facts,' she said quietly. 'But the Senhora de Ardo did say that she ran away from home after her mother died, and was ill after they found her.'

'She probably knew the details of the accident,' said Dacio, with equal quietness. 'But she may not have known that her parents had words and that Isabela was in a raging temper a few moments before she fell from her horse.'

Rosary stared at the portrait and thought to herself that it must haunt Dom Duarte, for he had been the first person to reach Isabela, the first to see her beauty ravaged by that awful fall to the cobbles of the stable-yard, where she had been trampled to death.

'Are you cleaning the portrait?' she asked Dacio.

'Yes. It used to hang in the main *sala*, but after the tragedy Dom Duarte had it transferred to the far end of the galley. Perhaps to be unreminded himself of her broken beauty, or perhaps to keep the child from being reminded that her mother was no longer a living presence in the palace. Last year, when she seemed stronger, he sent her to a convent school in Portugal, but as she pined to come home, he decided it would be for the best.' Dacio gave Rosary a long, deliberate look. 'I am glad. It has brought you to the island, and already your fair hair seems to light up these formal old rooms filled with their grand old furniture.'

'The *palacete* is a lovely place,' she objected. 'You with your artistic eye must see that.'

'My artistic eye, *senhorita*, prefers what is living and warm with emotion. For me there is nothing lovelier than a lovely woman.' He slowly smiled and thrust a

53

truant lock of hair from his eyes. 'I never dreamed that a tutor could be so nice ... or are you a modern young woman who objects to being called nice?'

'I am modern-minded up to a point,' she said. 'But I certainly don't object to being thought nice. I was brought up by my grandfather and he could be strict about certain things.'

'For instance?' His gaze dwelt on her lips as he spoke, at the full, soft curves of her mouth, lightly outlined by rose-coloured lipstick. 'He would not allow you to have friends of the opposite sex?'

'They were allowed ... as friends,' she said demurely, and meaningly.

'Are you warning me to keep my distance?' He moved his hand along the table top as he spoke, until his fingertips were touching hers. 'I am flattered rather than downcast; for I should hate to be thought harmless by a woman.'

'You Latin men are far from modest.' She transferred her fingers to the belt of her skirt. 'You have, in fact, an outrageous amount of self-esteem.'

'Perhaps this esteem arises from the fact that the Latin knows he is a man.'

'I don't doubt for a moment that you are a man, Dacio.' She began to walk away from him, along the gallery that had such a peculiar, sea-lit charm. Her lips held a smile, for it would be impossible not to find him a charmer. One would have to be very stiff-necked and frigid, and Rosary was neither of those things.

He fell into step beside her and he glanced down at her with a taunting, half-questioning look in his eyes. 'Are you an iceberg? I have heard it said of English women, and if it is so, and I must warn you that our island sun will soon start to melt you. Not to mention our music and our wine. May I invite you to a *festa*? I

54

have some friends who are soon to marry and there is to be a celebration, with music and dancing, and good food and wine? Will you come if I ask you?'

'I live under the roof of Dom Duarte,' she said. 'He informs me that he is my guardian, so you will have to ask him.'

'Then you will come?' Dacio spoke eagerly, and thrust again at that truant lock of hair that was so dark against the tanned olive of his skin. 'He cannot do anything else but agree. I am no stranger to him, and Lola will be at the wedding *festa*.'

'It sounds fun!' They reached the archway that led out of the gallery and Rosary stood there a moment, before bidding Dacio *adeus*. 'I will come if you'd like me to. When is it to be?'

'Next week! On the Saturday. Ah, how I shall be envied by the other young men!' Dacio gave a laugh that rang out boldly, wending its way along the corridor and bringing from one of the rooms a woman in a dark dress with high-swathed silvery hair who lifted her lorgnette on a silver chain and stared through the eyeglasses at Rosary and the young painter.

'I had better be on my way to the study.' Rosary walked away from Dacio, and murmured, '*Bom dias, senhora*,' as she passed her employer's disapproving aunt.

'*Senhorita*, you will wait a moment!'

Rosary paused and gave the *senhora* a polite look of enquiry.

The woman came up to her and studied the way she was dressed, the way she had her hair styled, and the light colouring on her lips. 'In this establishment, Miss Bell, the staff do not laugh loudly together, nor do I approve of paint on the face. You will remember in future to leave Senhor Cortez to his work, and you will at this moment go and remove the paint from your lips.'

Rosary stared at the woman as if she had not heard her correctly. 'I beg your pardon, *senhora*?'

'You will go and wash your face, Miss Bell. Neither my nephew nor I wish Gisela to pick up decadent habits from foreign women. Indeed, if I had my way——'

'I am fully aware of what you would do if you had your way, *senhora*.' Rosary was fuming with sudden anger. 'I don't know whether it's considered polite in a Portuguese household to insult people, but you have just insulted me. I have known for the past week that you have been awaiting the opportunity to find fault with me, and I am quite sure that when Dom Duarte returns you will lose no time in telling him that I have behaved like a loose woman with Senhor Cortez. You wish Gisela to be placed in the hands of an unintelligent martinet who will teach her to be as narrow in outlook and as joyless as yourself. Who will punish her for laughing when she shouldn't, and implant in her the idea that women are made for keeping house and being subservient to the man who has graciously agreed to take charge of her dowry, her person and her entire freedom!'

There Rosary broke off, and knew that by speaking out in this way she had lost her post at the palace. But she wasn't sorry. She had tried to be friends with this rigid woman, but it had been only a matter of time before they aired their mutual antagonism.

'Yes,' said the *senhora*, 'I shall indeed speak to my nephew about you. You should not have been allowed to stay here. I told him from the very start that you were unsuitable, and obviously insubordinate.'

'Senhora de Ardo,' Rosary's look became frankly

incredulous, 'I am not an unruly child to be scolded and rapped over the knuckles. I am a woman with a life of my own when I am not actually tutoring my pupil. Senhor Cortez was showing me the pictures in the gallery, not seducing me.'

'*Silenzio!*' The *senhora* lifted a hand as if to shield herself from such a downright expression. 'How dare you speak to me in such a way! You are insolent, and no lady——'

'I am a tutor, and even if I say it myself a darn good one. But obviously my ideas on how to teach a young girl to face life are a bit advanced for this household.' So saying, Rosary tilted her chin and proceeded on her way downstairs. She would carry on with her duties until summoned by His Excellency, and then she would tell him that if he wished his daughter to grow up to be a narrow replica of her aunt, then he must by all means allow the *senhora* to poison his judgement.

Yes, she would be perfectly frank with him before she packed her bags and said *adeus* to Vozes do Mar.

She caught her breath on a sigh ... it would be a shame to miss the wedding *festa*. She would have liked seeing a real island wedding, for she was sure not all Portuguese people were like the woman she had just quarrelled with.

She thought the study empty when she entered, and then Gisela slid out from behind the long curtains at the windows. She looked rather pale, and her eyes held a hectic brightness. Rosary knew at once that she had overheard that recent quarrel; Gisela knew also that her father would not keep a tutor who had upset his aunt.

'We had better start work,' she said briskly. 'I said yesterday that we would study the works of the romantic composers, starting with Chopin and going on to

Chaminade——'

'What is the use?' Gisela broke in. 'My father will send you away and whoever comes in your place will teach me dull things, and never laugh with me as you do.'

'I tried to hold my peace with the *senhora*, but she—well, you heard what she said, Gisela. I am not a painted flirt, but she implied that I was, and I'm afraid I had to defend myself.'

'Were you flirting with Dacio?' Gisela asked, and a look of jealousy flickered in her eyes. 'He is very good-looking and gay, and I have thought to myself that he would soon notice you and wish to charm you.'

'He was showing me the work he is doing in the gallery, and I found it most interesting. I can't ignore him just to please your aunt——'

'Did he show you the painting of my mother?' Gisela demanded.

'Yes—she was very beautiful.' Rosary spoke softly. 'You must always remember her like that, looking like a vision in her gorgeous red gown and her rubies.'

'I loved her,' Gisela said, 'but she never loved me.'

'My dear...!'

'She would never let me kiss her. She said children were a nuisance when they were young, and when they grew up they made a woman seem old. Now,' Gisela bit her lip, 'now she will never grow old, will she? My father and I can always remember her as proud and beautiful.'

'Yes,' said Rosary, but she was thinking of what Dacio had told her. Dom Duarte had knelt on the cobbles beside the dying figure of his wife, he had held her and seen her savaged face. That was the image he would always carry in his mind. 'Come, Gisela, let us settle down to our studies. There may be a chance that your father will consider I was justified in standing up to your aunt.'

'Yes,' said Gisela, 'if you speak with him before he sees Aunt Azinha. If you tell him how it happened that you had words with her.'

Rosary considered this and looked doubtful. 'I don't think he'd accept my word in preference to hers. I am still quite a stranger to him, and I believe he thinks my ways a little odd, as it is. You must remember that he put me on trial as your tutor, and now I have gone and called his aunt a narrow-minded and joyless woman!'

'All the same,' Gisela said eagerly, 'it can be arranged that you see him before Aunt Azinha has a chance to paint you a scarlet woman. Today he goes to the Courthouse, and he will be there all the morning. At noon he will lunch with Judge Lorenzo, and afterwards he will drive to Bahia de Roches——'

'The Bay of Rocks?' Rosary exclaimed. 'But why?'

'Because he likes to go there.'

'You mean the bay is a sort of getaway place for him?'

'Yes, that is how to describe it.' Gisela smiled. 'He is like other people and needs sometimes to be alone. Are you surprised?'

'I suppose,' Rosary shrugged, and gestured beyond the study windows to where the lawns lay like velvet, and where the white peacocks preened their plumage, lovely and strangely more exotic than their 'painted' kin. 'Your father is the overlord of the island, so aloof and certain of himself that I can't imagine him tramping a beach alone.'

'He may not be alone,' said Gisela. 'Sometimes I have known him to meet Lola there. I think he likes her and finds her attractive. But of course . . .'

'Yes?' Rosary coaxed. 'Tell it all.'

'If he married again he would have to choose a woman of position and good birth. That is the way of it with a man who has much property, and if he dies without a son to inherit, then a cousin in Portugal will be declared the heir, both to the title and my father's property in the south of Portugal. He has a castle there, and great vineyards, but it is the family tradition to govern Vozes do Mar for a number of years before the Duque feels free to return home.'

'I see,' said Rosary, and found it all very intriguing. 'So you believe your father would rather like to make Lola ... ah, but I shouldn't be gossiping about him in this way. It isn't ethical, and by this time tomorrow I may be on my way home! Dismissed for behaviour unfitting a tutor.'

Although Rosàry smiled, she was inwardly upset. It seemed so absurd that the *senhora* should rebuke her for being friendly with Dacio when Dom Duarte himself was more than friendly with the sister of the young artist. Of course, Lola was Portuguese, and the *senhora* was of the class that allowed its men to have their little distractions, so long as they were kept quiet and did not upset the traditions of the family. Rosary couldn't help but wonder how that unbending woman would react if her nephew decided to flaunt tradition and marry the vivacious Lola. Gisela had just said that he must have a son, and Lola Cortez did not look cool and passionless, unlike that lovely woman named Isabela.

'I—I don't want you to go away.' Gisela leaned against the piano and ran her fingers along the keys, producing a discordant sound. 'You understand me better than the teachers at the convent ... they said I was moody, but I am not so with you. Am I?'

'No, because I treat you like an adult, or almost. But what can I do, Gisela? If I beard your father at Bahia de Roches he may have Senhorita Cortez with him, and a man hardly likes an importunate tutor to butt in ... it would be disastrous, worse than being scolded by your Aunt Azinha! You are accustomed to your father. You can't imagine how he strikes a stranger.'

'He would not strike you!' Gisela turned her head and gave Rosary a startled look. 'Do you think he would?'

'No ... what I mean is that he is not like ... not like Dacio, for example. There are some people whom one accepts quite naturally. There are others who seem bounded by high walls of conventions, so that it seems hazardous to approach them.'

'Are you afraid of him?' Gisela asked.

'Not exactly afraid.' Rosary scorned the idea. 'Nor am I overawed by his title, it is just a feeling I have that a barrier exists between us, and it would be painful for me to—to plead with him.'

'Because your pride would be battling with his pride,' said Gisela. 'But if you really wanted to stay here you would not be afraid——'

'I'm not afraid!' Rosary insisted. 'I have never felt fear of anyone in my life, and the Duque is but a man!'

'There you are! He is but a man, and I dare you to go and confront him before he returns home and Aunt Azinha whispers like the serpent in his ear.'

'Gisela, you really mustn't say such things. Your aunt has her codes of honour, her bred-in-the-bone ideas, and I am alien to her. And I also think to some of the old women of the island. The other day as I walked in the village one of the old lace-makers crossed herself as I passed by her doorway. I wasn't wearing a scarf over my hair, and she looked at me as if—as if I were Eve!'

The young pupil looked at her young tutor, and they burst together into a sort of guilty laughter. 'Gisela, perhaps it would be best if you had a Portuguese teacher. Someone more attuned to the ways and the prejudices of your father's people——'

'No.' Gisela shook her head, and her eyes gave warning of temper and tears. 'I don't want to know only Portuguese things! To be told that I must grow up like my mother ... I want to be *myself*.'

'Of course you do.' Rosary put her arms around the girl and stroked her hair. 'And you shall. I'll talk to Dom Duarte——'

'Away from the *palacete*, Rosary, so Aunt Azenha won't know. If she knows, then she will find some other way to have you sent away.'

Rosary gazed with troubled eyes over the dark head bowed on her shoulder. She hadn't dreamed of becoming so personally involved when she had applied for this tutorial. She had merely thought it would be fun to work on an island ... fun! She was ashamed by her own flippancy. Cibby had insisted that she study human relationships if she meant to teach, so she would know in advance that each human being, young and old, had a problem. That it was part of humanity to be troubled by life, by the hope and expectation of love, and by the conflict that was a natural part of being in contact with other human beings.

It struck Rosary that she had almost looked upon this teaching post as a sort of holiday in the sun. It was the distress and tension which she felt in Gisela that made her realize the girl's innate loneliness; her need for companionship ... that little more than a teacher was asked to give ... that little less than a mother should give.

Rosary cupped the oval young face in her hands and raised it so her eyes were looking down into Gisela's. 'I promise you that I shan't be sent away, not if eloquence can help me to stay. How on earth do I find the Bay of Rocks?'

She learned that Amadeu the boatman would take her, if she paid him. He couldn't go out with the fishing crews because he had only one arm, but he made a living off the shellfish out on the reefs, and he also hired out his boat to young couples who wanted to be alone as they were allowed to be. He was considered chaperon enough, seated at the tiller, with his awesome empty sleeve and his patriarchal beard.

Gisela would not come, for it would be breaking her father's rule that she rest during the heat of the sun. So after lunch, and wearing white slacks and a sleeveless blouse of anchusa blue, Rosary set out for the weathered cabin on the beach where Amadeu lived. She found him idle and thought he looked more of a pirate than a patriarch as he argued about the price she should pay him for taking her to Bahia de Roches during his siesta.

'All right, here's the money!' She took some folded notes from the pocket of her slacks, and felt the flick of his eyes over her person as she handed him the money. She didn't like to admit to herself that he gave her a slightly creepy feeling, but she told herself he couldn't do much harm with that single arm of his busy on the tiller of his boat. It was tied by the little stepped jetty, its paintwork weathered but still as sturdy as Amadeu himself. Rosary took the seat facing the tiller, and as he cast off and sat facing her, she was glad she had worn slacks and didn't have to tolerate those wicked old eyes upon her legs ... she had not been all that aware of her own physical attraction until Erick Storn-heim had made her aware. Strange that youthful students did not possess the ability to make a girl aware of masculine danger; that mixture of indulgence and desire in the experienced male. She had mixed daily with students without ever feeling alarmed or curious ... and then one day Erick had looked at her legs and touched her hair, and she had suddenly come alive to the fact that men and women lived in different physical worlds, and that a girl was an object of desire to a man whether she liked it or not.

'So the *senhorita* wishes me to take her to the Bay of Rocks, eh?' Amadeu steered the boat with a brown and tensile hand which was probably as strong as two hands. 'It is a lonely place, not much visited by the people of the island. Long, long ago it was a wreckers' bay, and the bird cries sound like people lost in the water. Why would the English Miss wish to go there?'

'Just to see it,' she replied, in a cool voice. 'It sounds a most interesting place, and as you can see I have my sketch book with me. I should like to sketch you, Amadeu, if I may?'

He was flattered, and she had found to her secret relief a way to keep him quiet. Her charcoal pencil moved swiftly over the thick paper and as always it amused her to be able to capture the likeness of a face. It was one of those odd little gifts that did not inspire her to be an artist like Dacio. She knew her limitations, and her aspirations. One day she hoped to compose a lovely piece of music, but for now it was enough to be alive and young, and eager for the challenge of living.

'Why should such an educated woman come to our island?' Amadeu asked.

'Don't wiggle your beard,' she said, sketching swiftly that long black and silver badge of his seafaring years, forked and curling like a demon's. He must have been a devil as a younger man, she thought. Unruly-haired and black-eyed, making her wonder if he had lost that arm after a seashore fight over a wench, perhaps. He was a character, and still a rakish one.

'I am the tutor of the Governor's daughter,' she said.

'We all know it,' he said, 'and we all wonder why His Excellency chose someone so *d'ouro*.'

She felt his knowing gaze upon her hair, flaxen as the sunlight burning on the water, pale and shining looped back from her smoothly curving cheeks. 'You have my assurance that I came as a complete stranger to Dom Duarte. I applied for the post, but was not asked for a photograph. I could have been a stick in blue stockings for all he knew.'

Amadeu chuckled, 'The *senhorita* is quick with the reply, and men like it so. Better a wild heron than a tame goose!'

She had to laugh herself. 'Would you like to have this sketch when I finish it?'

'I hoped you would give it to me.' He was steering the boat towards a shoreline where the water beat in frills against large, strange-looking rocks. 'Is the *senhorita* meeting His Excellency at the Bay of Rocks?' Amadeu asked, in a sly voice.

'No——' She fought to look composed, for she might have guessed that the old sea-rover knew the comings and goings of everyone on the island. 'I am merely exploring the place, though I imagine Dom Duarte is always here or there, ensuring that all goes well with the island and its habitants.'

Amadeu looked at her with quizzical eyes, but he said no more as he gave his full attention to steering the boat to the shore, along a pathway of the sun that made the sea shimmer as if diamonds lay in thousands just below the surface. As they neared the rocks, they rode on the waves at the edge of the bay, a scimitar of rather dark sand studded with the green and gold rocks.

They passed skilfully between the barrier of high sea rocks, and the place was evocative of the savage past, and as the seabirds cried overhead they did sound strangely human.

The boat nosed the sands, and Rosary swept her gaze along that lonely stretch of beach, curving up and away into a tangle of tropical growth.

'I'd like you to wait for me,' she said to Amadeu, and she stood up and prepared to step on shore. 'You might as well take your siesta while I walk about.'

'It would be the discreet thing to do, eh?' He gave her an openly wicked look, and she thrust into his hand the sketch which she had made of him. She left him studying it as she jumped down on to the sands and began to make her way among the rocks to the incline. There seemed not to be a soul about, and she hoped that old reprobate wouldn't take it into his head to follow her. She quickened her pace, eager to see what lay beyond that boundary of tropic trees and veils of greenery. The air was warm, and heavy with the scent of creepers as she reached them and went in among them.

What was it that brought Dom Duarte here? A clandestine meeting with Lola Cortez ... or that touch of *saudade* in the soul of the Portuguese? That search for something beyond everyday living ... and everyday loving.

Rosary felt apprehensive, of seeing him with Lola, and seeing him alone. In both instances it would be an intrusion. He would be annoyed, and she didn't much fancy the annoyance of this man who, when he looked at her, and made her feel she had many things yet to learn about life.

She stood still as the cry of a bird touched her nerves. Perhaps she should turn back and not look for him ... but that would be the coward's way, and she had promised Gisela to do this thing, to find him and dare his temper, and insist on her right to be a human being in his employ, without the constant threat of dismissal because she spoke to Dacio, or laughed with Gisela and tried to make their studies a pleasure instead of a chore.

Sprays of orchids grew wild on the trees that formed this small belt of jungle and she was surrounded by the low-pitched shrilling of the invisible cicadas, folded in among the trees like living leaves. It was so cool and green, and then suddenly the sun struck down and opened a golden path out of the foliage, the bushes and ferns entangled in red and gold cane flowers.

She stood staring at a lonely sea-tower, with worn steps leading upwards in a spiral around that mossy relic of the past. Her gaze travelled upwards and her pulse beats quickened as she caught a slight movement on the stone shelf that encircled the tower, open to the elements and insecure-looking from the safety of the ground.

She knew instinctively that she had found the Dom's hideaway, where he came to enjoy the solitude of his own company ... or that of the attractive Lola. Rosary shaded her eyes with her hand, but she caught no glimpse of a bright skirt, and obeying instinct she made for the steps and started to climb them. It wasn't the tower she feared so much as the man who stood up there, but she was determined to speak to him about the situation which had developed at the palace. If she bearded him in this his lonely eyrie, then he would have to listen to her.

As she climbed higher and higher the wind off the sea caught at her hair and blew it about her face. The stone was hot from the sun, and so was the iron balustrade to which she clung as she climbed the last few steps. Gazing upwards to see if he had yet seen her, her foot caught against a broken step and she stumbled, and with a pounding heart she clung to the iron railing like a fly to a strand of dark webbing. She must have given a startled cry, for suddenly a shadow fell over her and Dom Duarte was standing there, looking down at her, but his face was as inscrutable as a mask of gold.

The wind tossed her hair, and she heard him say: 'What are you trying to do, break your neck?'

'Why, *senhor*, you!' She managed to sound breathlessly surprised. 'Fancy seeing you here of all places!'

# CHAPTER FOUR

'FANCY!' he drawled, and the next moment he had gripped her by the wrists and she found herself standing beside him on the sea-tower, with only the wheeling sea-birds in attendance. Her eyes dwelt on his face and they were filled with the eternal question asked by a girl when she finds herself alone with a man whom her instincts know to be more subtle than other men.

A girl could take a teasing line with some men and flatter them into being nice, but this man was different. He could not be easily charmed or cajoled ... his features were those of an autocrat; his touch was cool and steely.

He made Rosary feel unsure of herself, and aware that she knew more about music than men. That aspect of life had never really infringed. Romance had not yet entered her life, though she had been conscious when listening to a moving piece of music of something poignant as well as exciting in the prospect of love. Love should be like music, she had thought.

But having seen today a portrait of this man's wife she could not believe that love between him and Isabela had been like music ... unless one thought of Wagner and the high clash of temperament. Knowing about Isabela added to the tension of this moment, as if he would hate above all to have a stranger know that he came to this solitary place to pay penance to the memory of his wife.

Rosary felt the grip of his hands, the warning that he could hurt her if he chose to do so. 'What are you doing here?' he demanded, holding her with his eyes as well as his hands. 'Did you find this place by chance, or did you know that I would be here?'

'I—I knew you would be here,' she admitted. 'I had a reason for wanting to find you alone.'

'I see.' He studied her upraised face and still held her by the wrists, so she was unable to brush the wind-blown hair from her eyes. 'And how did you get here, Miss Bell? The Bay of Rocks is a long way from the *palacete*, so I presume someone brought you, either by road or across the water?'

'I came in Amadeu's boat——'

'Unescorted?'

'Of course, *senhor*. I'm not a child.'

'Exactly so.' His eyes swept over her and his fingers hurt the bones of her wrists, holding her firmly in the grip of shock as he went on relentlessly: 'You are no child but an extremely attractive young woman, with hair so beautiful that it should be covered, and yet if it were covered by the black lace which our women wear it would shine through as the sun does through shadow and shutter. I think you made a big mistake in coming here——'

'Here—to the tower?' she blurted.

For a long moment his face was sardonic and for the first time, here where the light was almost pure, she saw the tawny flecks in his eyes, tiny stabs of fire that might blaze with temper ... or smoulder with the passions of his Latin blood.

'I meant the island itself, Miss Bell. Why did you come looking for me?'

She flushed, for he made it sound as if she wished to be alone with him in order to flirt with him. The very thought of being caressed and kissed by him made her heart flutter with such panic that she attempted to pull her hands free of his touch. This instinctive action made her pull towards the edge of the platform, and at once he swung her back against the wall so that his tallness confronted her in almost a threatening way. 'You are too impetuous for high places,' he grated. 'It would not be much to my liking to have to write and tell your grandparent that you had a fall and broke your charming but impulsive neck. Now be still and tell me why you took this risk in seeing me alone.'

'I—I had to talk to you, Dom Duarte—before your aunt did so.'

'Ah, this sounds like an appeal! What have you been doing to upset the *senhora*?'

'It wouldn't occur to you, would it, *senhor*, that she might have upset me?' Rosary looked him in the eye and would not be intimidated by his superior strength, or by his position as Governor of the island. Only that morning he had been at the Courthouse listening to appeals of innocence ... now he could listen to hers.

'What have you done, Miss Bell, outraged my aunt's rather rigid sense of decorum? For instance,' his eyes agleam with sardonic humour flicked the white slacks she was wearing, 'have you been wearing trousers around the *palacete*?'

'I only wish it were only that, but she has near enough accused me of being loose and immoral because I wear a little make-up, and don't behave with monstrous false modesty in the presence of a man.'

'Which man?' snapped the Dom.

'Why, Dacio Cortez. We are both working at the palace and naturally we speak to each other. This morning your aunt chose to consider that I was behaving like a scarlet woman, and she told me to wash the paint off my face and to expect a summary dismissal from my job.'

'And what did you say, *senhorita*? I am sure you didn't retire from the fray without a retort or two.'

'I—well, I told her she was narrow-minded and joyless.'

'That was hardly the diplomatic thing to do.'

'My temper was up, *senhor*. I wear less make-up than some of the Portuguese girls I have seen during the evening promenade——'

'In my aunt's eyes they are village girls and have no connection with the etiquette of the *palacete*. She merely expects you to be discreet, Miss Bell, and to be an example for Gisela to follow.'

'I realize that, but do you think I overdo the lipstick? I have seen Lola——'

'We are not discussing the Senhorita Cortez.' Suddenly his voice was rather cutting. 'You are employed as a tutor and my aunt expects you to behave like one.'

'You mean I am expected to wear my hair in a bun, and to stare at the ground each time I happen to see Dacio?'

'What was he doing that induced my aunt to leap to the conclusion that you were not behaving with decorum? Were his arms around you? Was he kissing you?'

Rosary met the eyes that seemed to hold a certain scorn, and suddenly her temper was afire again, and despite Gisela she was strongly tempted to tell this man to take his job and give it to some straitlaced woman who would obey his rules without thinking herself a human being.

'If I wished to be kissed, *senhor*, I should want it to happen in a more secluded place than a gallery of your house! No, Senhor Cortez was not making love to me!

We were discussing his work in the picture gallery and your aunt merely needed an excuse to be disagreeable. She wishes Gisela to have a keeper rather than a friend, and that was why I risked seeing you in this unorthodox way. I promised your daughter that I would state my case to you before your aunt had a chance to distort the whole thing.'

'And do you imagine I would listen to a distortion of facts without consulting you or Cortez?' The question had the cool smoothness of ice, but the eyes that penetrated Rosary were flickering with tiny points of flame. 'I am aware, Miss Bell, that your personality is a little too vital for the approval of my aunt, therefore I shall make up my own mind about your continuing suitability as a tutor for Gisela. Tell me, has the child any real feeling for the piano? Her mother used to play.'

Feeling somewhat startled that he should mention his wife, Rosary took a moment or two before answering him. Then she said quite honestly, 'Gisela has a light and pretty touch and I can help her to improve as a musician, but the depth of true talent isn't there. Is that what you hoped for, *senhor*?'

'Quite frankly, no. I have made plans already for Gisela's future and I don't wish for a career daughter. It is enough that her talent can be made socially pleasing. We Portuguese have not yet succumbed to the pop music of your country and we still enjoy a Chopin *étude*, or a Latin lament.'

'I enjoy those things as well, *senhor*.' A smile came and went on Rosary's lips. 'I am far from being a pop music fan, and I do assure you there are still people in my country who enjoy real music. We have not all gone crazy.'

'I am relieved to hear it.' Amusement played over

his features, softening for a moment the stern lines of his mouth. Rosary felt, then, the attraction of the man, for there was something in herself that couldn't help but respond to that proudly held black head, that high-arched nose, those bold satanic eyebrows. He was born to command and she was too feminine not to feel it.

'So you came to the Bay of Rocks in the boat of Amadeu, eh? You are not easily intimidated, are you, Miss Bell? I wonder, in fact, what it would take to make you nervous. What do you think of my sea-tower?'

'It's solitary, rather dangerous and evocative. A place to which a person would come to meditate.' And to dwell on the past, she thought. 'I should apologize, *senhor*, for disturbing you, but you do understand my motive? I don't wish to be sent away merely because your aunt has taken a dislike to me. It is far more important that Gisela likes me.'

'Do you feel you are good for my daughter, Miss Bell?'

'Yes. I have awoken her interest in several things since I came to Vozes do Mar. After all, you just intimated that you don't want a vegetable for a daughter. You want one who will glow in Portuguese society, and these days it isn't enough for a girl to be merely pretty.'

'You think Gisela a pretty person?' And he seemed to dwell on the words with the same deliberation that his eyes dwelt on Rosary's silk blouse of anchusa blue, and her hair that held the hot sunlight. He studied rather than looked into her eyes that were deep and warm as cognac.

'She promises to be a beauty, *senhor*, and she should

have personality to match her looks as she grows into a woman.'

'The cask should hold wine and not soda water, eh?'

'Exactly, for when the cask begins to wear what is left?'

'That is rather a quaint philosophy for such a young woman. At your age you should be thinking of only the romance in life.'

'But, *senhor*,' she said demurely, 'as your daughter's tutor I am not allowed to be romantic.'

'But, *senhorita*,' he mocked, 'you assured me that you were only talking of work with the good-looking Dacio.'

'Yes, in working hours,' she agreed. 'But as your employee would I be allowed in my free time to think of romance?'

'I see no harm in thinking of it, but as I have said before it would be advisable, while you are here on the island, to conduct yourself more like a Latin young woman than a free-thinking British girl.'

'I notice that you make a subtle distinction, *senhor*. Do you consider Latin girls are more sensible than I am?'

'Let us say they are less impulsive than you are.' He gestured at the breakneck view from the sea tower. 'I have never known a girl of this island to climb those precarious steps to this high and windy place.'

'Not even Lola——?' The words were spoken and could not be recalled, and Rosary felt her pulses leap as he looked at her between narrowed eyelids. She had come here with the intention of conciliating him, and yet she seemed driven by some wayward reaction to his personality to make him annoyed. It was a foolish and dangerous thing to do, for they were very much alone and he seemed a man who wouldn't hesitate to punish an offence to his dignity.

'For a second time, Miss Bell, you seem to imply that I arrange secret meetings with Senhorita Cortez. Are you merely young and curious, or are you deliberately provoking me by prying into something which has nothing to do with you?'

'I—I have never supposed for a moment, Dom Duarte, that your affairs are anything to do with me.' Her cheekbones seemed to burn and she felt like a small, impudent girl under his gaze. 'I only wondered if Lola had ever wanted to see the view from this height. I should imagine that it takes in most of the island.'

'From the other side one can see the countryside. Come, let me show you, and be careful of that iron railing. The stonework of the tower is old and in places the railing is not as secure as it should be.' As they made their way to the other side of the tower Rosary could feel, like a fine steel manacle, the grip of his fingers about her left wrist. He was treating her as if she were little older than his daughter, and far less tractable.

They stood side by side gazing over the land that undulated far below them. Rosary saw the flutter of snowy egret wings above the green rice fields. The revolving sails of the windmills, full-bodied and catching the sunlight upon their shafts. Field workers could be seen, the women with the lower part of the face covered in the oriental way. There were clusters of small white houses, with chimneys that flared into turrets, almost like miniature castles, castles and minarets. The palm trees and tropical vegetation, the hot sunlight on shimmering water, completed a picture that Rosary couldn't help but fall in love with.

'Vozes do Mar is a lovely island,' she murmured. 'I don't want to leave it, just yet. That was why I put my pride in my pocket and came to find you alone, *senhor*. I am not the flirt your aunt would like to make me seem. I am a good tutor and given half a chance I can do a good job.'

'You hope to soften my heart of stone, eh?'

'If you had such a heart, Dom Duarte, you wouldn't care if your daughter had music or not. You may have a stern heart, but that is a different thing.'

'How different, *senhorita*?' Though he had warned her about the iron railing he leaned an elbow on it himself and regarded her as she stood there beside him, her pale hair blown to one side of her face by the wind, leaving exposed her left ear, the fine curve of her neck and her youthful, flawless skin.

'Stone cannot be softened, it can only be broken, or it can break.'

'But you believe that a stern heart can be softened, eh?'

'I like to think so.' She gazed straight ahead of her and tried not to be so overpoweringly conscious of his eyes, knowing they had slipped from her profile to her shoulder, bared by the softly curving blue of her blouse. It was strange that a man so aloof should make her so aware of herself.

'You are optimistic as well as impulsive, Miss Bell. What if I said that I don't believe for one moment that the intentions of Cortez are impersonal with regard to yourself? What if I thought it wise at this stage to send you home before that young man becomes too *simpatico*?'

'Really, *senhor*, do you think I am so unused to young men that I shall lose my head over Dacio? I studied alongside male students at my grandfather's school, and I learned to keep a level head, and not to take flattery as a declaration of love.'

'Cortez is Portuguese, and the tongue of the young Latin is smooth and varied as the *azulejo*.'

'Does it grow less smooth as a Latin male matures?' she asked, with a wicked demureness.

'The Latin becomes more skilful, more practised, *senhorita*, just as a musician does if he has at the start a gift for playing on the senses.'

'Are you trying to make me feel afraid, *senhor*?' She gave a laugh, for he mustn't know that it was he, not Dacio, who could make her feel unsure of herself. Power and charm ran together in his very bones, and combined with his fatal marriage they made of him a man no woman could possibly ignore, or take lightly. He had depths to him upon which a young man like Dacio bobbed like a buoyant cork. Rosary knew that for a girl there was danger in being drawn into those depths ... dark, fascinating and painful.

'Life can be tragic, Miss Bell. Men can be cruel ... women can be hurt. None of this has yet touched you, therefore you are vulnerable, a term you might repudiate being a modern-minded English Miss, but all the same a valid one. What would you do right now, for instance, if I felt the impulse to kiss you?'

'But you wouldn't!' She turned intensely shocked eyes to his face. 'It would be against your principles as the man in command! You are bound to set a good example——'

'But we are here alone, Miss Bell, and did you not say that you would choose to be kissed in solitude?'

'Yes—I said that, but I didn't mean that I would submit to any man, regardless of my feelings. I'm not a girl who kisses lightly, even if you are a man who does so!'

'Be careful, Miss Bell.' Suddenly his hands were spinning her to face him and he held her by the waist, like something he could snap in two with the living steel of his fingers. 'You might be speaking to a man who makes the tears of women his wine.'

'Y-you shouldn't threaten me,' she gasped. 'Why are you doing it, to test my morals? To see if I am the sort of girl to lose her head over the Governor of Vozes do Mar? Or over any man ... as your aunt suggests?'

'I am naturally curious about a young woman with hair like a blaze of pale silk, and eyes that hold the dark-gold fires of the topaz. It seems unusual that a girl so attractive should choose to be a tutor on a remote and foreign island. Can it be that you have come here to escape from a man?'

In that instant Rosary could have told the exact truth, that there was no romantic love in her life, but the physical closeness of this dark and compelling man acted like a spur to her frightened senses. She thought of Erick and the way he had looked at her the last time they had met. She reached out in panic to Erick because she had known him since she was a schoolgirl.

'I'm not running away from a man,' she said. 'We thought it would be a good idea to be apart for a while, so he could concentrate on his career as a conductor of music. I am sure you realize that while a man is making his name as a musical conductor there should be no other distractions.'

'And Vozes do Mar is many miles from London, eh? The young man cannot be tempted away from his career by the topaz eyes?'

'No, *senhor*.' She felt a terrible fraud, and yet she felt secure in the knowledge that he would never be likely to meet Erick. She could now pretend to be 'spoken for' and being a rigid Portuguese he would respect that invisible barrier. There had to be a barrier between them, for when he came close to a girl he was much too devastating. Now when she looked at him the mockery was gone and his face was once again a cool bronze mask, with above it the windblown sable hair. She didn't dare to look at his lips, for she dared not be curious about his kiss.

'Soon the afternoon will be over and we must return to the *palacete*.' His hands slipped away from her waist and she almost shivered at the coldness that encircled her body in place of his touch.' You will come with me, of course. I can't allow you to be alone with Amadeu as twilight falls. He is an old pirate and not to be trusted.'

Rosary didn't make the obvious answer, that for several tense minutes she had not trusted Dom Duarte himself. '*Senhor*, your aunt will know when she sees us together that I have pleaded my cause before she has had time to condemn me.'

'Then I will let you leave the car at a side entrance and you can slip in through the back way. There is no harm in being discreet, eh?'

'I would prefer it, *senhor*. Until she decides to accept me.'

'Be as discreet with the young artist, Miss Bell.' There was a sudden note of hardness in the deep voice. 'And now shall we leave our friends the birds and go to the car?'

'What of Amadeu?' she asked. 'I told him to wait for me.'

'He will not wait all night. Come, Miss Bell, and be careful of these steps as we descend. I notice that you wear the sensible sandals, at least, and not those high heels which seem to make a woman walk as if upon unbroken eggs.'

'I always understood, *senhor*, that men preferred women to be uncomfortable and helpless.'

'Even men, *senhorita*, are becoming less barbaric in their taste.'

She wondered about that as she walked ahead of him down the winding steps and heard the cries of the birds with less distinction. He had a silent way of walking, as if his every muscle was controlled and supple as that of a tiger. The skin seemed to tighten at the nape of her neck and she could feel his eyes upon her, alive with those tiny tawny lights. Today she had learned how his wife had died ... and she had learned also that she was capable of a fabrication in order to keep him at arm's length.

As she reached the security of the ground she gave him a look from wild-fawn eyes and felt the impulse of the fawn to flee into the underbrush. It was crazy! Never in her life had she felt so potently this sense of danger ... of seduction. It was as if the island air from way up there had gone to her head like wine, and now with her feet on the earth her legs felt trembly. Because of it, because he was the heart and cause of this awareness that made her silly and weak, she turned on him. 'But you don't like to see a woman in trousers, do you, Dom Duarte? That is too much a sign of female emancipation.'

'Or dissipation,' he drawled, and he stood over her, tall, sheathed in his perfectly fitting suit like a rapier in its scabbard. 'Untidy hair and trousers make me think of a slut.'

Her head shook, as if he had slapped her. Her eyes blazed ... and then she hated him and the intoxication was gone. 'Your cruelty is really highly refined, isn't it, Dom Duarte?' she said, and knew exactly what she was going to say next. 'I wonder if you will ever forgive yourself for the words which killed your wife?'

'No,' he said coldly, 'I shall never forgive myself. Nor shall I forgive your audacity in raking over the ashes of memories private and painful to me.' And as he spoke, and the island light was caught and held in his eyes, she saw the flare of pain as he remembered as only he could that shocking moment when Isabela had been thrown from her sable mount, the beauty kicked from her face. Rosary could have cried out, then, that she was sorry ... achingly sorry for what she had said, but he walked past her, among the trees, and she followed him in silence, and knew that now he must send her away, for how could she stay and be unforgiven by him?

He reached ahead of her the strip of road where the Porsche stood waiting, its bodywork agleam under the rays of the slanting sun, which now held a gleam of red as the afternoon began to die.

Dom Duarte opened the passenger door and Rosary slid inside the car without looking at him. She was beyond understanding herself, and she sat withdrawn in her seat, staring ahead of her as he took the wheel and the car shot away from the roadside with speed and elegance, and flashed through the reddening sunlight along the undulating road that cut through the centre of the island, dividing the countryside from the sea. Rosary turned aching eyes to the sea and it shimmered and seemed to be running with the life-blood of the dying sun. It was so painfully beautiful that she gasped, and only then did she realize that she was pressing a hand to her throat as if to hold back her stricken apology which he would treat with all the scorn it deserved.

How long they drove in silence she never knew, but dusk was painting the palace with shadows when the car came to a halt at a side entrance and Dom Duarte told her, curtly, to get out. She obeyed him and was about to close the door behind her when he said:

'What has been between us this afternoon had best be forgotten, but I would ask you not to discuss with Gisela the way her mother died.'

'I—I wouldn't dream of doing so.' Rosary clenched the handle of the car door so hard that a fingernail broke. 'I will pack my things tonight—I expect you would like me to leave in the morning?'

'Don't be so childish!' he snapped. 'I am not so cruel that I would deprive you of your living in order to punish you for having an opinion of me. You may continue to work with Gisela, and I will tell the *senhora* that she must show more understanding of your ways, which are naturally different from our own. *Até a vista*, Miss Bell!'

It was so cool, so indifferent, till we meet again, and Rosary felt a chastised child as she slipped through the side entrance and heard the Porsche speed on towards the front of the palace, where it would make a smart turn in against the steps...

There her breath caught in her throat as she heard a sudden scream of brakes, a crashing of glass and a tearing of metal. In an instant she was running in the wake of the car and as she entered through the forecourt gates she gave an involuntary cry of horror. The Porsche was overturned against the steps and the entire front of it was a mass of spinning wheels and shattered glass from the wide front windows. Even as she ran she saw oil and petrol snaking like dark blood along the tiles of the forecourt ... she knew that Dom Duarte was trapped inside the overturned car and at any moment the tank was going to explode. She heard the crunch of the glass as she stepped on it and her hands reached blindly for the shoulders that jutted from the door which had been forced open by the crash. She tugged and pulled, and was vaguely aware of someone running down the front steps of the house. She felt the *senhor* stir, and then another pair of hands were helping her and they had pulled him free, and they kept on pulling, with desperate urgency, as a tongue of flame leapt and the next moment engulfed the car in a hot sheet of fire that lit up the front of the palace

Dom Duarte gave a groan and stirred again where they laid him. Blood was running down his face, and in that nightmare moment it seemed to Rosary that tragic history was repeating itself ... and then his eyes opened and he was staring up at her and she saw the tips of the flames reflected in his eyes.

'You will be all right.' It was Dacio who spoke. 'You braked too late and crashed into the steps.'

'M-my head is humming.' He stared a moment more at Rosary's shocked white face in the blazing illumination of the burning car, and then he fainted away.

When the doctor came hastily to the *palacete* it was found that Dom Duarte had concussion, several badly bruised ribs and a badly wrenched left ankle. That his injuries were not worse was a miracle, and everyone drew a shaky breath of relief when Doctor Rivas reported that the *senhor* had been made comfortable in the master bedroom. Gisela broke down and cried after her ordeal of waiting for the doctor to descend from her father's bedside. She shook with sobs, and when the *senhora* told her to control herself, for after all her father had not been killed, the girl turned on her and said stormily that she was stony-hearted and thought of nothing but correct behaviour and never giving way to human feelings.

As the hot, broken words struck at her, twin flushes appeared on the rather gaunt cheekbones of the *senhora* and her eyes bored into Rosary like daggers of accusation. *She* was being blamed for Gisela's very natural display of emotion, and hastily, before anything more could be said, Rosary led the distressed girl from the *sala* and upstairs to her room.

'C-can't we peep in at him?' she begged. 'Just to make sure he is all right?'

Rosary hesitated, and then decided that it couldn't harm Dom Duarte, who was sleeping now, and would put Gisela's mind at rest. Together they made their way along the gallery upon which his master suite was situated and very quietly she turned the handle of the tall door and glanced inside. His valet was seated on a chair near the bedroom door and he rose at once when he saw Rosary and came quietly across the carpeted floor to where she stood with Gisela.

'May we see him, Manoel?' Gisela caught at the valet's arm. 'We shall be as quiet as mice and won't make a murmur to disturb him.'

Rosary didn't speak, for suddenly she couldn't. She felt as though her heart were in her mouth, and she dreaded even as she desired to see the man whom she had helped to drag from the wreckage of his car. It had seemed like a bad omen that he should crash like that ... driving in a temper.

When Manoel beckoned them to the bedroom door, Rosary hung back. Gisela immediately caught at her arm and she had to go with her, into that big, silent, darkly furnished room where Dom Duarte lay sleeping, his black hair ruffled and damp and showing the edge of a dressing over his brow. His features looked more chiselled than ever, and distant as a rather beautiful mask.

Those moments beside his bed were so strange, so unreal, and as Rosary saw the breath stir his lips, she thought how angry he would be to be seen in this helpless state by her, who had reminded him only a short while before the car crash of his wife's painful death.

As Rosary backed quietly away from his bed, she knew that his mind had been upon Isabela when he had failed to apply those brakes in time. She turned and walked swiftly from his suite, stricken by the guilt of knowing that she had helped to cause the accident which could so easily have killed him.

# CHAPTER FIVE

FOR several days the atmosphere at the *palacete* was subdued and anxious. There was no way of keeping Gisela's mind on her lessons, so Rosary gave up the struggle. She knew the girl was haunted by the loss of her mother, and she hung about near her father's rooms, and even Dacio could find no way of amusing her.

The only relief was that the accident had taken the *senhora's* mind off her feud with Rosary, and for the time being she seemed to become more human. Her nephew was one of the few people she was fond of, and she took upon herself the task of nursing him. She carried trays to his room, soothed his brow with iced water and made sure no one disturbed him.

As soon as possible he was up and about again, but his ankle was still painful and he used a walking stick with a polished knob to assist him in getting about the small palace, and his large study where the letters were piled up and the telephone kept ringing to ask his progress, and when would he be fit enough to attend to this matter or that. Dr. Rivas insisted that he remain at home for at least a week, and during that time Lola came often to the *palacete* to keep him company.

After seeing them together, strolling the sunlit lawns or sitting in cane chairs, Rosary was convinced that the Latin girl was in love with him, but as usual it was impossible to fathom the true state of his feelings. But always with Lola he seemed charmed and amused; a smile clung about his lips, and he wore informal shirt and slacks, and the stick that aided his limp gave him a subtle attraction. It also gave Lola the excuse to prop a stool under his ankle whenever he sat down, and she obviously enjoyed waiting on him.

In the evenings Lola and her brother were invited to dinner, and in the salon afterwards the *senhor*, with an air of laziness, would request that Rosary play the piano for them. Immediately she would turn to Gisela and suggest a duet, and she would feel the mockery in his eyes as they played together. He knew, with all his devilish shrewdness, that she was shy of playing alone for him. The others didn't matter; they were not so demanding as he.

Then one evening it came, the quietly spoken yet definite demand for a solo performance from her.

'I am sure you are acquainted with the Chopin *études*,' he said, leaning back in a comfortable chair, with a glass of cognac in his hand and a glint of the diabolical in his eye. 'They are too complicated for Gisela at present, and I feel in the mood for the E Major Etude. Do you know it, Miss Bell, and can you play it?'

Rosary had refused cognac and held instead a small cup of the rich dark Portuguese coffee. There was a long-tailed bird painted in lovely colours on the cup and she gave it her attention as she replied that she knew the music but she was sure she could not do it the justice the *senhor* would expect.

'I shall make allowances for any mistakes,' he drawled. 'I realize that the *études* are complex under their veil of beauty, but the mood is set for such music, with the lamps glimmering and the scents of the night stealing in from the gardens. Come, *senhorita*, you owe the invalid his whim.'

She looked at him, then, and wondered if his words held a double meaning. She owed him more than a whim, for they both knew that she was partly responsible for that dark bruise concealed by the sweep of his hair, for the strapping across his ribs and the pain he still felt in his ankle. He smiled slightly as she looked at him, and she glimpsed the tantalizing challenge in his eyes.

'Do play for us,' urged Lola, with the assured gaiety of a girl who could do no wrong in the eyes of the man who sat near to her, so that the dark formality of his evening suit was a foil to set off the rose brocade of her long dress. Her glossy hair was looped back smoothly from her brow, and she looked a madonna by lamplight, softly glowing and desirable.

'Yes, do give us a treat,' Dacio encouraged. 'I have heard you teaching Gisela her scales and arpeggios, but you have never yet played seriously for us. Are you shy?' he added wickedly.

'No,' she said, but she was nervous in the presence of Dom Duarte when he chose to play the spotlight of his attention upon her. He did it mockingly (she could see that) but to everyone else he appeared the quintessence of courtesy. The master of the house, flattering the tutor by requesting that she play for him a favourite piece of music. Rosary could feel everyone looking at her. The hands of the *senhora* paused beneath the lamp where she worked the silver hook into the strands of crochet silk. Gisela stopped stroking the tabby kitten which had been given to her by the lean young gardener with the face of a boyish Byron.

Everyone seemed motionless, and then Dom Duarte asked Dacio to open the piano for Miss Bell. With resignation she arose from her chair and walked across the salon, with its sheen of long curtains framing the terrace, the dark gloss of the antique furniture, and the carpet woven with gigantic flowers. Against the

89

panelled walls glowed watercolours as fine as silk, and baroque carved cabinets held books, and things of porcelain and silver. She arrived at the piano, an Empire grand of ivory white and gilding, with reclining ivory figures holding the candelabra. The top was opened and the candles had been lit by Dacio, and she felt his breath stir warm against the nape of her neck as he arranged the padded seat for her and she sat down.

'Don't be nervous,' he murmured. 'Even *he* cannot eat you.'

She cast a side-glance at the artist and suddenly she smiled. It was true. Dom Duarte was only a man, and she had played for Erick who was a conductor of music, and he had applauded her.

Dacio melted into the shadows and she was alone, isolated at the superb piano, with the candlelight sheening her hair, and etching in soft silver and shadow the slim lines of her figure, and the curve of her wrists as she laid her touch upon the keys and willed herself to forget the man who watched her with eyes that flickered with points of gold ... hawk's eyes, waiting narrowly to swoop on her faults and punish her for daring to be the only female on the island who didn't fall over her own feet in a rush to please him.

The *étude* he had asked for drifted from the tips of her fingers with all its haunting magic, and in the midst of it a nightingale awoke in the garden and began to sing. She was so thrilled that she forgot her audience and she played on and on, rippling into a scherzo, joining the iridescent notes of the bird with those of a nocturne, wandering without thought into the soul of a waltz. What brought her back to earth was the realization that she was playing a melody of her own. She broke off in the middle of it, and as if by magic the nightingale stopped singing, and someone laughed, breathlessly. Gisela came running to the piano, where she bent to hug Rosary. 'You were marvellous! Do go on—please!'

'No——' She was suddenly all nerves and her wrists were pounding with her pulse beats; she couldn't have played one more note tonight. 'I've done my party piece!'

She jumped to her feet and faced the others almost with defiance. 'I hope I didn't make too much of a fool of myself,' she said.

'A fool?' It was Dacio who stirred in the shadows, who almost groaned the words. 'That was beautiful.'

'It was delightful,' Lola broke in, but even as she smiled there seemed a flash of resentment in her eyes, as if she had been secretly hoping that the English girl would spoil the music and reveal herself as inept.

'It was spellbinding,' said Dacio, determined to have his say.

'*Obrigado*, Miss Bell,' said the man who had challenged her to play. 'I did not recognize that final piece, which you ended so abruptly. May I know the composer of it?'

'I—I forget, *senhor*.' She couldn't tell him that it was something of her own, half realized in the last few days, singing through her blood and flashing from her fingertips during that sweet-wild duet with the nightingale. 'It's probably a sentimental tune I picked up from a film, or a radio serial. A piece of airy nonsense that sticks in a girl's mind.'

'Perhaps,' he murmured, and his eyes flicked the wisps of hair that clung to her temples, and the soft heat of her skin. 'Take a seat and cool down, Miss Bell. We have enjoyed your music and you must be rewarded. Would you like a glass of wine?'

'No—thank you.' She shook her head and the swing of her hair fanned a light breeze against her flushed skin. 'I think I'll go out on the terrace, if you don't mind? Just to catch my breath.' She caught at the skirt of her blue-grey striped silk dress and brushed past his chair, hastening into the cool night air, out of sight of the room with its soft lamplight making a halo around that dark polished head. Was it possible that she was the faintest bit disappointed because he had not been the one to praise her playing; to say it was spellbinding ... that it had beauty? She rested against the stone parapet and she could smell the roses that clambered against the latticework of iron that scrolled the terrace. The nostalgic scent of the roses reminded her of home, so many miles away from this Portuguese palace on an island, with its people whose ways were so subtle they seemed to heighten one's sense of the dramatic.

The men here were not given to that robust laughter of the Englishman, and they smiled with a charming gravity that hinted of the mysterious. There shimmered under all exchange with a woman a hint of passion, and that *saudade* of theirs, that longing for the perfect romance.

Or the perfect woman!

She stood where the terrace branched away from the salon, and the darkness was softly broken by the glimmer of the stars. The air she breathed was an intoxicant, like wine, and it wasn't chill but softly warm, and her thoughts turned to the sea and swimming in the starlight. Her breath quickened and the longing to swim ran in sudden tumult along her veins.

Why not? If she went quietly, while the *senhor* and his guests still talked in the salon, there would be no one to see her, no one to ask questions, or to suggest that it was improper and the sort of thing a Portuguese girl wouldn't do. But first she must collect her swimsuit and her wrap, and to do so she must slip past the salon windows and enter the house through the drawing-room windows. She turned and was about to hasten back along the terrace when she was brought to a standstill by the lean figure of a man, his white tuxedo glimmering in the soft darkness.

'Dacio—what do you want?' She was impatient with him because she wanted to get away, to play truant in the sea all by herself.

'Aren't you pleased to see me?' He sounded rather hurt. 'I wanted to say again how much I enjoyed your music. It was a revelation.'

'A revelation of what?' she asked. 'Surely the grand-daughter of a famous music master should be able to play a few tunes on the piano?'

'Don't belittle your gift.' He advanced towards her and made her retreat to the parapet. 'Modesty can go too far, and though it might suit His Excellency to have you the self-effacing tutor, it doesn't suit your personality, or please my sense of beauty and art. You must know, Rosary, that you have a disturbing quality. Even your name hints of a secret place where roses might grow, and where bells might softly ring.'

'You're kind to say so, Dacio, but if you were to see me in England you would think me quite ordinary. I seem unusual because I am the only English girl on this island, among so many raven-haired, dark-eyed *senhoritas*.'

'Rare would be a better word.' He stretched an arm and enclosed her within a niche of the terrace, among the roses and their night-drawn scent that was more sensuous than the scent of other flowers. It wasn't the beauty of the rose alone that inspired men to send them to the woman desired. The velvet petals held

93

within them the magic power to stir the senses, and Rosary was aware of this as she looked into Dacio's dark eyes and saw their admiration.

'I—I was about to go to my room,' she said, then panic quickened in her as he came a littler nearer. 'Dacio, we can't be alone like this! The *senhora* doesn't approve, and she has threatened already to have me dismissed if I am seen flirting——'

'Are we flirting?' he murmured, and his eyes sparkled darkly in his handsome face. 'Are you enjoying it?'

'Dacio, do you want me to lose my job?' she tried to push away his arm, but it was solid, well-muscled, the arm of an artist who was accustomed to holding a brush and palette for hours at a stretch. He had the diabolical patience of the artist, as well, and she knew herself trapped by him. There was only one way to get him and herself off this terrace before they were seen and their position was misconstrued as a lover-like one.

'To tell you the truth,' she said, 'I was going to fetch my bathing things. The night is so warm that I want to go swimming.'

'Are you inviting me to go with you?' he asked, a note of pleasure running in his voice. 'I should be delighted! As a Latin male I have never enjoyed swimming at night with a girl.'

'What about swimming trunks?' She was committed now, and besides he looked so boyishly pleased, and she could well believe that he had never indulged in the adventure of a late night swim with a Portuguese girl; too many family restrictions were imposed to allow of it. Also, the very idea of defying Dom Duarte appealed to Rosary ... so long as it was done in secret and he didn't find out.

'We must be quiet about it, Dacio,' she said. 'I have to slip into the house for my swimming things, and you must fetch yours. I suggest that we meet in about fifteen minutes on that narrow path that leads down to the *palacete* beach.'

'I shall be waiting!' He quickly took her hand and brushed it with his lips, and for a moment she wondered if she was being altogether wise in going with him to the beach, where they would be alone.

'You will behave yourself?' she demanded. 'I mean to swim, not to indulge in a—a flirtation.'

'You are afraid I shall make love to you?' he said, half smiling.

'I'm not afraid, but I shall be annoyed. It will spoil our friendship, Dacio, for I shan't speak to you again.'

'I believe,' he murmured, 'that the British are more prim than the Portuguese.'

'We have our codes,' she agreed. 'A friendship and a love affair are very different things.'

'And you want my friendship, eh?'

'Yes, I need a friend. See you in a while, *amigo*.'

'*Ate a vista, amiga*.'

She hoped he meant it when he called her *amiga*, and she smiled as she sped swiftly and silently along the terrace.

She made it from the palace without being detected and they met on the path that was narrow and steep in the darkness. Hand in hand, and stifling their laughter, they made it to the beach, where the bathing *caseta* was situated, fitted out with a couple of changing cubicles, a lounger of cane with a matching table, and a cabinet in which there were glasses and bottles of orange and lemon squash to quench the thirst after a swim in the sea.

Dacio must have had his trunks on under his slacks, for he was ready and waiting when Rosary came out of the *caseta*.

'Such a night!' he said, and his head was thrown back in a sort of pagan worship of the stars that were so brilliant above the sea that the beach was lit to a soft shimmer by their light. There were clusters of palm trees near the water, their fronds spread gracefully to catch the starlight. The air was tangy with island spices and foliage which had been sun-drenched all day.

'Race you!' she said, and she sped past him down the beach to the creaming surf, gasping with delight as the water splashed high about her legs. She struck out with a laugh as he dived in behind her, and she heard him call out to her that she had forgotten to wear a cap.

'I never do,' she said, for the water streaming through her hair gave her a lovely free feeling.

'You are a naiad.' He was alongside her and they swam in unison through the dark sapphire sea. 'You are glad I am with you?'

'Yes—it's lovely swimming at night, isn't it? More primeval than in daylight.'

'Have you ever said a thing like that to any other man?' he asked, and she saw the glint of his teeth as he turned his head to her, and she felt all around them the illimitable loneliness of the sea. They were two specks in that ocean, and yet they were far more. They were a girl and a man, and she had not yet been awakened to all it meant to be a part of the plan that made life as eternal as the sea. Curiosity stirred and she wondered about desire. She knew the facts, but the feelings had so far eluded her.

Exhausted at last, they turned and swam back to the

shore, and she felt the sea ripples curling about her toes, and the water streaming from her hair as they walked across the velvety sand and flung themselves down with their backs to the palm trees. She knew he was watching her as she wrung the water from her hair and tossed the long damp tail over her shoulder. She knew that her minutest action was of interest to him because he had known only Portuguese girls and they didn't behave with such a lack of modesty in front of a man. They were always superbly groomed, almost sedate, and their conversation was aimed to flatter rather than to provoke.

Shades of the harem lingered in the Latin girl, and more than a hint of the Moor lingered in the men!

'Do you suppose your sister will guess that we're together?' she asked. 'You are usually there to take her home.'

'His Excellency will perform that duty, and I am certain he will enjoy it. You must have noticed that when he looks at Lola he is less of the hawk and more of the dove.'

'Your sister is lovely, Dacio. Have you ever painted her? She's so vivid that she makes me feel like a water-colour.'

'You?' he laughed, and played his toes against her toes. 'If you knew anything about painting you would know that the vivid colours are more tiring to the eye than cool colours. Do you know that under the stars, in their reflection from the sea, your skin is as mysterious as the covering of a water-bud. You are the girl I should like to paint dressed in a slip of silk from your bare shoulders to your knees.'

'Like a harem slave?' she quipped, but her fingers dug deep in the sand with the realization that if Lola guessed they were together she might mention it to

Dom Duarte. She experienced a feeling of consternation mixed with defiance. The chemistry of these Latins made the most innocent action seem meaningful, as if design and not loneliness had brought about this starlight swim with Dacio.

As if Dacio guessed the trend of her thoughts, he leaned a little forward and said teasingly: 'What is your opinion of the man who rules Vozes do Mar? Do you consider him a tyrant who likes women to be demure and obedient?'

'I think he finds it a bit infuriating that I am not in the habit of bending the knee to any man, not even a *duque* with a pedigree of great distinction and power to go with it. I don't tremble at his wrath or blush all over at his smile. I,' she filtered sand through her fingers and made a little pyramid of it, 'I don't think he likes me very much, but he knows Gisela does like me, and that is the important thing.'

'How can you be so sure that you aren't liked by him?' Dacio studied her face, washed clean and pure by the sea, with little hollows under her cheekbones, and eyes too candid to hold the secrets of a sophisticate.

'A girl can always sense these things,' she replied.

'Then your senses must have told you that I—like you.' He scattered the pyramid she had made and smiled directly into her eyes. 'On the other hand it isn't so easy to tell whether I am liked by you. The English girl is direct in some matters, but strangely reserved when it comes to her feelings. It is, indeed, a paradox that our Latin girls should be bodily guarded and yet be less shy of letting their eyes reveal their emotions.'

'Latin eyes are very expressive,' she said. 'You said yourself, Dacio, that the hawk's eyes of the *senhor duque* are more dove-like when he looks at Lola.'

'Do you envy the favour she finds in the *senhor*'s eyes?' he asked, teasingly.

'I'm not the envious sort, thank heaven. I was taught by my grandfather to count my blessings, which may sound old-fashioned, but it's something I believe in. A sound body and mind are prizes beyond a pretty face.'

'A very Puritan outlook, Rosary, but right now you look far more of a naiad.' Dacio's look travelled from her tousled hair to her bare shoulders, and down her slender body to her bare and sandy feet. 'You are not cold? If so I will fetch your wrap.'

'No—in any case we must go home soon. It must be quite late.'

'Stay a little longer, until the *senhor* has seen Lola to the door of the villa.'

'Doesn't he enter for a nightcap?'

'No—a man cannot do that if a girl's guardian is absent, and he is not yet her official *novio*. Our rules of courtship are quite strict, and a girl's reputation can be ruined if she allows a man to break those rules.'

'Then you and I must have broken a dozen in the past hour,' Rosary laughed. 'What a good thing I am not a Latin girl. If we were seen my reputation would be in shreds, alone with you like this, in my bathing suit.'

'You might be so compromised,' he said deliberately, 'that I would be obliged to marry you without delay.'

'How awful for you, Dacio!' Her eyes danced in the starlight.

'*Deus*, it would be thrilling if you and I were forced to marry by the edict of Dom Duarte! Shall we allow ourselves to be discovered?

'No!' She leapt to her feet as if stung, gave him a startled look, and then fled to the *caseta*. She knew he was giving chase even though she couldn't hear him on the soft sand, and she ran breathless into the little beach house and slammed the door in his face. Lord, that was all she needed, to be compromised into marriage ... forced into it by the feudal laws still prevalent on this island. She snatched her wrap and quickly put it on, belting it tightly about her waist. She slipped into her sandals, regardless of the sand grains between her toes, and parcelled her dress and underclothes under her arm. Then she hastened out of the back door of the *caseta* and ran all the way up the path to the grounds of the *palacete*. Out of breath and with a stitch in her side she hurried through the gardens, where statues lurked like pale figures, and trails of leaf and flower brushed her face like ghostly fingers.

When she reached a side entrance that led into the hall by way of an arched corridor she had to pause to catch her breath. Night enshrouded the palace and overhung its turrets. From here no lights could be seen and she breathed a sigh of relief. She could slip in unobserved and be safe in her room within three or four minutes. Silently, feeling the sand grating against the soles of her feet, she made her way along the corridor and tried the door to the hall. Her heart slumped, for the handle turned back and forth with the impotence of a handle attached to a bolted door.

She might have guessed that at this late hour the various doors leading into the *palacete*, with its various treasures, would be bolted against possible intruders. She stood biting her lip. If she banged on the door and made herself heard by one of the servants, the incident would be bound to be repeated to the *senhora*, who liked to know all that went on in and around the precincts of the Governor's residence. She would demand to know why Rosary came to be locked out, and the end result would be an argument. A refusal on Rosary's part to be treated like an adolescent who must account for her every movement.

Rather than face the inevitable inquisition Rosary decided to return to the *caseta*. Dacio would by now have left, and she would sleep there and pretend in the morning to have gone out for an early swim. It was known that she sometimes did this, and she would avoid having to explain how she came to be locked out ... like a little cat who had been out on the tiles!

Upon arriving back at the beach house, after a stumble on the dark path which grazed her arm, she found the place deserted and quickly entered, closing and bolting the door behind her. She switched on the light and after securing the back door she felt more at ease. She also felt rather hungry and found in the drinks cabinet a small barrel of biscuits, which she dipped into as she set about making the lounger as comfortable as she could. There were cushions and a rug, and after she had dressed she felt warmer. She tried not to think of the dark beach all around the *caseta*, but when she turned out the light and sought her makeshift bed, she could hear the rustling of the surf, and the whispering sound made by the fronds of the palm trees as a breeze blew in over the water.

She snuggled down under the rug and her wrap, and had to smile at her own British craziness. If she had gone sedately to her room after leaving the salon, and if she had not impulsively asked Dacio to go swimming with her, she would at this moment be tucked up cosily in her bed at the palace. Safe under its turreted roof and not alone like this, with strange night sounds whispering at the doors and windows.

She felt the throb of her bruised arm as drowsiness

crept over her. Something in the air of this island had an odd effect on a sensible career girl, and never before had she played a Chopin *étude* with such a rare understanding of the music.

As the tree-frogs croaked in unison with the rippling surf, she drifted off to sleep.

# CHAPTER SIX

Sun and ocean splashed the beach as Rosary came out of the *caseta* and stretched herself after a somewhat restless night on the lounger. She took deep lungfuls of the fresh morning air, and was uncertain of the time because she had left her wristwatch in her bedroom last night, when she had collected her swimsuit. The surf flung itself high up the sands, and the sun was swinging in an arc across the beach, like a golden blade.

It would be about six o'clock, she decided, which would give her ample time to stroll back to the *palacete* with all the casualness of the early riser who had gone for a swim and was returning with hunger for the coffee and rolls which the chef would be preparing. The day always began quite early at the residence, with the arrival of the *senhor*'s secretary at eight o'clock, and the *senhora*'s supervision of the cleaning, bed-making, dusting and cooking. For each day there was a different menu, and everything had to run smoothly in order to cope with the people who had appointments to see Dom Duarte.

Rosary made for the path which snaked upwards among the trees, and she glanced at her arm and saw that it was now darkly bruised ... a memento of an evening which would have been totally without significance had it occurred back home in Sussex!

She made her way around a tree that was bursting with flower, and one of the great passion-blooms swung against her cheek and spattered dew in her eyes. She paused to brush away the moisture and when she fully opened her eyes again someone was standing on the path ahead of her, facing her, motionless in white trousers and a black polo shirt, leaning slightly on a black stick.

She stood shocked, unmoving, for he was the person she had hoped above all to avoid, and already he was searching her with sharp eyes that in the morning light were like ebony dipped in ice. Her heart beat quickly and her knees felt weak. She had to speak, and she had to sound as casual as possible.

'*Bom dia, senhor*. The water's grand this morning. You ought to try it.'

'You are saying you have been swimming, Miss Bell?'

'Yes,' she replied, even as a tiny warning bell rang in her brain, and he regarded her with eyes that accused even as they ran over her, from her wicker sandals to her crumpled dress, upwards to her hair. In an instant her heart thumped and each nerve in her body seemed to be a separate alarm signal. Her hair wasn't wet, or even damp. It was tousled and uncombed, and she knew from the flare to his nostrils that he wouldn't believe her if she said she had worn a cap. He *knew* she had not been swimming this morning.

'Why do you bother to lie to me?' he asked coldly, and as he spoke he came towards her, limping slightly, and then suddenly he raised his stick and slashed the head off a passion-flower. There was a rain of petals and dew, and Rosary winced, as if he had struck her. His eyes glinted as they followed the flight of her hand to her mouth, holding back a cry. When he stood over her she could feel the anger vibrating in him. Such anger made her afraid, for it told her that he knew about last night.

She wanted instantly to rush away, to be among

other people, so he would be forced to control his temper. She could pass him on the path if she moved quickly enough ... but even as she moved he caught her by the arm with his free hand and half swung her against the tree that was heavy with its burden of passion-flowers.

That little cry of fear escaped her and she looked at him with the shaken look of a girl who had never before in her life been treated so savagely. Her hair had flung itself across her face, and the bark of the tree acted like barbs that clung to the thin material of her dress. Her great brown eyes impored mercy of a stern face and cold eyes.

'Last night,' he said grimly, 'Gisela was stricken with one of her nightmares and I heard her cry out and I went to her. She was upset and she wanted your company, so I went to your room to fetch you. You were not there, Miss Bell. Your bed was undisturbed and had not been slept in. I at once looked for you, and when it became apparent that you were not to be found at the *palacete*, I telephoned Senhorita Cortez to ask if you were at the villa. She said no, but she thought you might be in the company of her brother.'

At his mention of Dacio, and the way he looked at her untidy hair and her crumpled dress, not to mention the bruise that his fingers had touched when he had flung her against the tree, made a scorching flush run all over her body. It left a flare across her cheekbones and sparks in her eyes.

'You have been out all night!' he accused.

'And what do you imagine I've been doing, Dom Duarte? Roaming the tiles like some immoral little cat?' The words would not be controlled and her indignation was such that she could have hit him, lashed out like a little cat at his scornful mask of a face. How dared he judge her, and accuse without justification? She hated him for looking at her as if she offended him.

'I demand to know what you have been doing!' Suddenly his hand was gripping her shoulder, and his lean fingers were grinding the fine bones beneath her skin that bruised easily.

'You're hurting me!' she spat at him, but when she tried to twist away the pain intensified, and his look was that of an inquisitor who would torture the truth out of her.

'You have been in the company of Cortez, haven't you?'

'And what if I have?' she said defiantly. 'What are you going to do about it, *senhor*? Dismiss me from your precious island ... expel me like a criminal because I have a perfectly normal desire for a little freedom when I am not tutoring Gisela? Is it then a crime under Portuguese law for a girl to take a swim at night?'

'So it was last night that you went swimming?'

'How clever of you to guess, Dom Duarte!'

'You are an impertinent and foolish young woman who deserves to be spanked!' The flare of his chiselled nostrils told her the extent of his fury, and the bite of his fingers warned of the Latin violence that could master even him, the Governor of the island who should at all times be in control of his passions. 'You will tell me how you spent the remainder of the night ... I demand to know!'

'Your demands are insatiable,' she retorted. 'I must be discreet, demure and deferential at all times. I am English and free, but I must pretend to be a Latin girl, chained by the wrist to male authority. I am over twenty, yet I am treated as if I'm an irresponsible child!'

'And I suppose by Cortez you are treated as a woman of the world?'

'Are you curious, *senhor*, or are you collecting evidence that will prove me guilty of fast behaviour?'

'I am warning you, *senhorita*, that if you persist in answering my questions with impudence, I shall treat you as you appear to want to be treated.'

'And how is that, *senhor*?'

He stared down into her eyes and she saw again those tiny flickers of tawny fire. 'If you think, Miss Bell, that it is safe to provoke me, then you are very much mistaken. If you would like a demonstration of how unsafe it is, then just persist for five minutes more in acting the liberated female returning from a night of free love.'

'It is you,' she cried, '*you* who choose to think I spent last night in Dacio's arms!'

'Only because I am goaded into it. My first concern is that you might have been hurt ...'

'Do you really expect me to believe that?' She gave a laugh, which turned to a cry as he gripped her arm and studied the bruise that was dark against the paleness of her skin.

'You did not have this when you played the piano last night, so it must have been inflicted after you left the salon and disappeared for hours on end.'

'If you are thinking Dacio did it, then you are mistaken. I—I fell over on the path to the beach and knocked my arm against a tree. It was dark ...'

'You were running away from the young man?'

'No – I found I was locked out of the *palacete*, so I came back to the beach and spent the night in the *caseta*. And I spent it *alone*, Dom Duarte.'

'I know,' he said coolly.

'What? You put me through this inquisition and now you tell me that all along you knew I was alone?'

'Naturally. But there comes a time, Miss Bell, when headstrong young women need to be given a dose of medicine which might help to cure them of rash behaviour. You flounced out of the salon last night with all the pet of a *diva* who has not been praised as highly as she believes she should be. You play quite beautifully, Miss Bell, but even in that you are swayed by impulse and emotion. You won't be mastered by the dictates of the music ... or by those of a man, will you?'

In all fairness he was right about her playing, and he was overwhelmingly correct when he said that she wouldn't bow down to the dictates of a man at any cost. She tossed her head. 'How did you know I was alone at the beach house?'

'I sent two of the menservants to search for you, and again I telephoned the Cortez villa. This time Cortez himself answered my call, and Alfredo found the *caseta* locked and the marks of small sandals leading through the sand to the door. He carried a torch, of course. He hasn't eyes that see in the dark, and when he reported back to me I advised that you be left alone to sleep until the morning.'

'And when morning came you came looking for me in order to lecture me?'

'Don't you think you deserve a lecture? I hired you to be Gisela's tutor and companion. When she needed you last night you were not available. It is unfair to charm someone into becoming dependent upon you, *senhorita*——'

'I am not a female Svengali,' she broke in. 'How was I to know that Gisela would have a nightmare? I didn't even know that she was subject to them.'

'She has been so since her mother died.' He paused, and his fingers slid away from her shoulder, and his eyes left her face to brood upon the shimmer of the sea below the path on which they stood. The scent of the passion-flowers was distilled as the sun broke through the trees and dried the dew on the clustering petals.

'I think,' he went on, 'that last night her nightmare was triggered off by my own recent accident. Gisela has not your independent spirit, Miss Bell. She needs to be secure in the affections of those she loves. Be always within call another time, if you wish to keep your position as tutor to the child.'

'I am not to be dismissed, then, for my breach of conduct?'

'It cannot really be helped,' he shrugged, 'that you respond to the impulses of your British blood and your sense of adventure. I, too, have felt the call of the sea on a starlit night ... but I am curious as to how you persuaded the young Cortez to return to the villa ... like a good boy?'

Such was her relief at the sudden lessening of tension between them that she relaxed against the tree and as she remembered how she had bolted from Dacio she broke into a smile. 'He said if we were caught alone, *senhor*, you might insist that I marry him. Knowing how strict you Portuguese can be when it comes to the protocol between the sexes I decided that I didn't wish to be married against my will.'

'Such a procedure would hardly suit the young man in England, eh?' Dom Duarte leaned on his stick and the look he gave her was a sardonic one. 'Whoever this young man is he wasn't quite wise to let you out of his sight. He could not have known that Vozes do Mar has on certain people the effect of a full glass of *vinho verde*, which can go to a young head like champagne.'

'Yes ... I mean there is magic here. A lost-in-time atmosphere.' She spoke almost with shyness, for it seemed that only in a temper had they really talked, and it felt strange and confusing to allow him into her thoughts. 'It's hard to believe that beyond the sea and the mountains there is a world in which people fight with weapons, and trample carelessly on all the ideals of the saints and the reformers. I think if I were Portuguese I should never want to leave this island.'

'But you are not Portuguese.' His eyes flicked her hair, the fair strands of it tousled about her triangular face that without being beautiful had a charm of its very own. A dash of spirit about the mouth and chin, shading to a fey quality when it reached her cheekbones and her large eyes with their oblique corners. 'You are a girl without artifice, Miss Bell. You say what you think, and this is a quality which we Latins find a little disconcerting.'

'You prefer to wrap everything in silk ... or steel,' she dared to say.

'That is the Saracen in our blood,' he agreed, and in his eyes there lurked a smile, a curious smouldering together of those tawny lights.

'And the Saracen in you likes women to be submissive to your wishes, *senhor*.'

'It makes life a little smoother for a man to bear, *senhorita*.'

'But to be entirely placable is to be entirely boring,' she retorted. 'And you don't quite convince me that you don't enjoy an argument with a woman.'

'We call it a duel of words,' he slightly mocked, as if her reference to herself as a woman amused him deeply. Yet she was but a year or so younger than Lola, and he seemed to take seriously the remarks and feelings of the Latin girl. It could even be that he was planning to make Lola Cortez his second wife, for no man so vital as this one could stay solitary for ever; nor could he remain always in a state of penance. Rosary bit her lip, for the one and only thing she regretted saying to him was that he should never forgive himself for the words which had helped to kill his wife.

Life was complicated ... she had never known how deeply so until she had come to live among these people who lived a great deal of the time on their emotions.

'I—I should be getting back to the palace,' she said. 'Gisela may require me——'

'She will ask where you were last night. You will of course tell her the truth.'

'Yes, *senhor*. But what of the *senhora*? She will think——'

'She will be told that Alfredo and I found you alone and asleep at the *caseta*.'

Rosary stared at him. 'You said Alfredo found me——'

'Naturally I was with him.' Dom Duarte's face was quite unreadable; that mask of bronze that forbade questions. 'I have a second key to the beach house and the door was unlocked so that I might make sure you were all right. You were sleeping, but the rug had fallen to the floor. I covered you up, and then I left, locking the door again. I have while you are in my employ a responsibility towards you.'

'I suppose you have.' She flushed slightly. 'I seem to be causing you far more trouble than a Portuguese tutor would. I—I suppose I ought to say I'm sorry, but in England an employer wouldn't be so concerned about a straying tutor.'

'That is one of the effects of female liberation in your country, Miss Bell.' He gave her a sardonic bow to emphasize his words. 'But as a Latin I don't yet regard a girl of twenty as my equal in wisdom ... ah, your eyes flash at me a look which says I have not always been wise. This is true, and if I can make mistakes how many more can a mere girl make! And now shall we go and have breakfast? You must be feeling hungry.'

'I am,' she agreed, and as she fell into step beside him she was aware of his height. He was very much taller than Dacio, and the other men she had seen about the island, and this intensified his air of authority. Perhaps long ago the blood of some captured Anglo-Saxon girl had mingled with that of the Saracen ancestor from whom sprang the Montqueiros, passing down the centuries the look he had of a proud dark hawk.

They came to the palace gardens and walked among the high and scented camellia hedges, the bushes of geranium and banks of deep-toned azalea. They crossed the *patio* tiled with the raised designs that caught the sunlight and glittered with oriental beauty. Above were the balconies that enclosed the rooms in intricately twisted iron.

Rosary's eyes were as startled as her heart ... why had she never noticed before these subtle hints of the east in tilework and iron, and the incense of camphortrees and weeping peppers? Small birds of paradise flew about in the trees and winged about the hanging lamps in the cloistered archways. Suddenly she felt so out of place in her crumpled dress and uncombed hair that she couldn't wait to get under the shower in her private bathroom and wash from her skin and hair the sand grains that still clung to her. No wonder this man of cultured taste had looked at her with such offended eyes.

'I must go and get changed before I eat breakfast,' she said, and she stared at a mass of moon-daisies and avoided his gaze. 'If you had decided to send me away this time, *senhor*, then I shouldn't have been surprised. I did behave impetuously——'

'Quite! And be assured that there are times when I feel I should dismiss you. Look at me when I speak to you!'

She reluctantly did so, but her mouth rebelled against the reproof in his voice. She pushed from her eyes a strand of her truant hair and a ray of sunshine caught the action. 'You are a disturbing influence, Miss Bell. A young catalyst, I think, rather than a little cat. Now go into the house and have your breakfast.'

She fled, hastening through the door that last night had been locked against her. She ran lightly across the hall and up the stairs, glad that she reached her rooms without being seen. There with an acute sense of relief she stripped off her slept-in clothes and was soon under the shower and lathering herself with almond-oil soap. Now, with the warm refreshing water cascading through her hair and down over her body, she could reflect on her talk with Dom Duarte, and the amazing fact he had revealed without direct intention.

Last night he had led the search for her, and he had found her sleeping in the *caseta*. The rug had fallen from her, he had said, and he had covered her up.

She blinked the water from her eyes, stepped out of the shower and rubbed herself down with one of the huge soft towels that were always folded over the warming bar. Against his will he had revealed another small facet of his complex personality. He could be concerned for even a tutor, and he could be kind ... but he could also demonstrate that a steely thread of the master ran through him. A little shiver ran through Rosary as she recalled his slashing of the passion-flower with his stick.

In the circumstances she was lucky not to have been dismissed from her job, for he had rooted out without any effort the cause of her rebellious behaviour. She had played really well last night, but all he had said was, '*Obrigado*.' As cool and polite as if she had recited *An Ode to a Primrose*! instead of playing the Chopin *études* which involved technical complexities only a music student could be aware of; she had seen young male musicians go white with vexation at not being able to master some of those subtle, beautiful traps laid by the master of the piano, Chopin himself.

Had it annoyed the *senhor* that she should end her recital with a piece of music invented by herself? He had known, of course, and that was why he had asked her in such smooth tones to name the composer.

As Rosary buckled the slim belt of her short doeskin skirt, and pulled her soft green shirt into place, she heard her bedroom door open and when she turned to look Gisela was standing there, rather pale and unsmiling.

'Hullo, my dear. I'm ravenous for breakfast and shan't be more than another minute.' Rosary felt almost a guilty quickening of her nerves as she buckled her still damp hair at the nape of her neck, and decided not to apply lipstick but to look the scrubbed and shining penitent at the breakfast table. 'Isn't it a lovely morning, Gisela?'

'Where were you last night?' the girl demanded, leaning back sulkily against the door. 'I wanted you and you couldn't be found.'

'I went for a swim and like an idiot I got locked out.' Rosary spoke nonchalantly, for she wasn't going to be 'tried' a second time for what, after all, had been only a minor crime. Much as she tried, she couldn't react like a Latin and these people must come to terms with the fact that for twenty odd years she had been behaving like an English girl and only for a few weeks had she been here, among people whose customs and restrictions were new and strange to her.

'You were with Dacio,' Gisela accused, and in that moment her likeness to her father flashed like lightning across her face, but her eyes were stormier, her temper less controlled. 'I suppose you like him better than you like me because he's a man! I suppose you wanted him to make love to you!'

'Nothing of the kind, Gisela!' Rosary was sparked to anger herself. 'I seem for ever accused of being a flirt by members of this household. I begin to think that I should put my hair up in a bun and wear a pair of big horn-rimmed spectacles, not to mention a sack of a dress!'

'You'd still be too pretty not to be noticed,' Gisela muttered, and then suddenly she ran to Rosary and threw her arms around her, almost squeezing her breathless. 'I'm frightened of losing you, that is why I am mean this morning. I—I know that as one grows up, young men do become important, and I shall try not to mind too much if you care for Dacio. He is handsome——'

'Gisela, I am not in the least in love with Dacio Cortez.' Rosary smiled and stroked her pupil's dark hair. 'We're friends, that's all. It really is possible for a young woman to be friends with a man, even though you Latins disbelieve it and attribute only romantic reasons for a girl's enjoyment of a man's company. I had friends among the students I trained with and found it stimulating to argue with the male of the species. I also found that I was cleverer in some ways than the lordly creatures, and I certainly never bothered to flatter any of them, unless I admired this one or that for his musical talent. Now, before I buckle at the knees for the want of nourishment, let us go down and eat breakfast!'

Friends again, they sped laughing along the gallery and down the stairs, where they were brought up short by the appearance of Dom Duarte from his study. He was dressed impeccably in grey, a sure sign that he was going out on business.

'You look brighter this morning, *pequena*,' he said to his daughter. 'Good morning, Miss Bell.' His smile was bland and courteous, and showed not a sign of their recent battle of words ending in a truce. 'I am going into town and if the two of you will quickly eat breakfast I will take you both with me and we can lunch – after I have attended to a certain matter—at a restaurant. After all, it is Saturday and life should not be all lessons.'

Gisela stared at her father. 'Do you mean it, *senhor*?' she asked, pleased and amazed, and a little flushed beneath the smooth olive of her complexion.

'Have you ever known me, Gisela, to say anything I did not mean?' The look he gave his daughter was teasing. 'A small outing to make up for the nightmare last night.'

Gisela glanced eagerly at Rosary. 'You want to go?'

'Well——' Rosary was a trifle uncertain and her eyes met the *senhor's* as if seeking his assurance that she was wanted. 'It would be nice, but I don't want to be in the way——'

'Miss Bell, I did mention that I would take both of you to town,' he said, looking suave. 'We will choose an open-air restaurant so that you won't need to dress with more formality. I shall be waiting in the car for you both.'

He limped away in the direction of the courtyard, and Gisela caught like a happy child at Rosary's arm. 'Let us quickly eat! He doesn't like to be kept waiting too long and we don't want him to go without us, do we?'

'No,' said Rosary, but as she sat down to hot rolls and jam and creamy coffee she had the sure feeling that having shown her the stern side of his personality Dom Duarte was now going to prove how disarming he could be. The prospect was daunting, for she didn't doubt that his charm was matched by his autocracy.

'I hope this skirt and blouse will do for a run into town?' she said to Gisela, when they had taken the edge off their hunger.

'You look nice, and very English.' Gisela wiped jam from her lips and jumped to her feet. 'Are you ready?'

'Yes—I'm just finishing my coffee, but if we're going where there are shops I must go upstairs for my bag.'

'Then do be quick! I will go and sit in the car with my father.' Gisela dashed off as if she expected to have this unexpected treat snatched from her. Rosary went upstairs to her room, where she combed her hair into a chignon and applied a little make-up. She wanted to look as cool and poised as possible, and as she sprayed on a little of her Tweed perfume, she prayed that she wouldn't say or do something which would rekindle that spark of discord which seemed to smoulder between herself and the *senhor duque*. It was something she had never encountered before ... this chemical reaction of her spirit in opposition to a man's.

Arriving in the courtyard she found the chauffeur waiting beside the grey limousine, with Gisela and her father seated together on the wide back seat.

'Please to join us, Miss Bell.' The *senhor*'s gaze

**117**

flicked her hair and her softly reddened mouth as she stood there by the door which the chauffeur held open; she knew that something glimmered deep in his eyes as she stepped inside and felt the deep carpet underfoot and the plushy softness of the wine-coloured upholstery. Never in her life had she travelled in such a handsome car, which seemed to glide on the air itself as they sped along the road which bordered the *palacete*. The morning was filled with sunlight and the sound of birds, and for a mile or more the car ran beside the boundary wall of the residence before branching on to the public highway.

'I don't believe you have yet seen a lot of our township, Miss Bell.' Dom Duarte spoke with a smile of such charming courtesy that Rosary was left speechless for a moment or two. Was this really the same man who had thrown her against a tree and spoken so bitingly to her only a couple of hours ago? It was really unfair of him to be able to switch so adroitly to courtesy while she was still smarting from his attack, and feeling rather bruised where his fingers had gripped her, under the green silk of her shirt that made her skin seem so white in comparison to his and Gisela's.

Gisela wore a lemon-coloured shirtwaister that contrasted brightly with the soft olive of her skin. Her eyes were sparkling and she looked really pretty.

All of a sudden Rosary relaxed. She knew that the *senhor* thought her an infuriating young woman with a will of her own, and somehow the knowledge added zest to this outing. She would pay him back by being so demure that he in his turn would be disarmed, and to start the ball rolling she gave him a smile that Cibby always called her melting one. It was a smile which started in her eyes and spread slowly to her mouth, so that it took on the likeness of a slowly opening flower.

'I am wondering, *senhor*, if it will be possible for you to show us the historic houses and buildings of the island's township. I am sure some of them must be many years old and adorned with those colourful tiles such as are used in Portugal itself. They depict legends and the voyages of your Portuguese explorers, don't they?'

He half quirked an eyebrow at her request and gave her what she termed to herself 'an old-fashioned look'. 'After I have completed my business it should be possible for the three of us to take a tour of the antique houses left intact over the years,' he said. 'Are you becoming interested in the history of our island, *senhorita*?'

'How can I help it, *senhor*? I am sure one of your own ancestors must have been responsible for discovering Vozes do Mar ... of even naming it, perhaps.'

'Have you been studying our family records and bound letters in the library?' he asked.

'No, *senhor*, but I have the feeling your family has its roots deeply embedded in the history of the island, and firmly bound up in its future.'

'None of us can be certain of the future,' he said, 'but it is a fact that a Montqueiro was the discoverer of the island and its first Governor. As he listened to the sound of the sea from the deck of his caravel, as the water rippled to and fro against the shore, he seemed to hear it whispering and in his log book that very night he wrote that the new acquisition of Portugal should be named Voices of the Sea.'

'A romantic notion, *senhor*.'

'Yes, *senhorita*,' he agreed, half mockingly. 'We are a people in whose soul dwells the illusion of happiness, heard like a whisper in water and never fully grasped.'

'Aren't you happy?' Gisela caught at his hand and pressed it to her cheek, and with a little laugh he turned the palm and kissed it.

'I speak in the abstract, little one. The very young, like yourself, can grasp at a joyful hour as if it were tangible. I am afraid adults have to ask the reason why this moment they are glad, the next moment a little sad.'

'I could not bear it when you had your accident.' Gisela looked at him as if for ever she would absorb his face into her memory. At nine years old she had learned that loved ones were mortal, and she clung to his hand as her eyes clung to his features. 'I was so afraid ... one of the nuns at the school used to say that the departed call the living to them!'

'It is over, Gisela!' He spoke firmly. 'The accident was entirely my own fault, and we have Miss Bell to thank for risking the flames on my behalf.'

Abruptly he looked at Rosary, and though his eyes were inscrutable he was smiling slightly. 'I had not forgotten that you came to my aid.'

'I—I'm glad your injuries were not more serious, *senhor.*'

'I'm rather glad of that myself, *senhorita,*' he said drily.

# CHAPTER SEVEN

THEY entered the old *palacio* of administration, now used as a museum, by a picturesque gateway wrought into the many intricate patterns employed by Moorish craftsmen. Long ago the walls would have been pure white, but now they were heavily patched with lichen and sprawling vines, and bent in almost a bow of welcome was a catalpa tree—the tree of heaven—casting shade as they passed beneath its branches.

There were no other visitors but themselves and it seemed to Rosary that they were entering a place half haunted, lost in the past, for the inner patio was dark green with creepers and the fountain that was like a miniature minaret no longer played its liquid music, and its tilework gleamed with a certain malevolency through the mosses that cloaked it. There was a *chafariz* attached to the wall, used long ago for filling the household pots, a gem of antiquity, which awakened in the ready mind of Rosary a picture of gazelle-eyed girls tripping there in their bare feet, veiled to the eyes, to drink from its spout.

They entered the hall of the *palacio* through a doorway chiselled in a smooth oval out of the stone, above which perched a black raven, a pet of the museum-keeper perhaps, which gave a croak but otherwise did not stir, watching them intently as they studied the relics and treasures from another time, the Saracen armour that was fearful in itself, the costumes and jewellery of Portuguese nobles, the beautiful hand-made dolls and the fans that had flattered the Latin language of the eyes. There were gemmed weapons and exquisite scent bottles, and the two girls hung over them with the enthralled feminine worship of lovely things that had been handled long ago by lovely women, living half-captive lives.

Their feet echoed across the tiles of the floor, an arabesque of patterns that glowed like the old lost colours of an eastern carpet. From the ceiling hung lamps enclosed in delightful cages of wrought iron, studded with gleaming stones that would have shafted a myriad of jewel colours down upon the faces of the women and men who had gathered here in another time, clad in velvet and brocade.

The walls were panelled in *azulejos* that depicted the colour and spectacle of *festa*, both pagan and religious. The fun of grape-treading, and the full-sailed ships in which the Portuguese captains had sailed on their voyages of discovery.

The tile pictures, mainly in gold and indigo blue, were so detailed, so full of story, that Rosary could have spent the entire day just wandering around and absorbing the history and strange charm of this place.

Suddenly the raven croaked loudly and she turned with a quick smile to eye the bird. 'The raven of St. Vincent,' she said, and felt Dom Duarte quirk an eye at her, as if surprised that she knew a little Portuguese history.

'"*And his eyes have all the seeming of a demon's that is dreaming,*"' she quoted the words, still looking at the bird of dark plumage, still looked upon by the man whose own darkness was so intensified by the grey smooth suiting that he wore. '"*Tell me what thy lordly name is on the night's Plutonian shore!*"'

'He is an apt guardian, eh, of a place such as this where every "*silken sad uncertain rustling of each purple curtain*" thrills "*with fantastic terrors never*

122

*felt before!*" The *senhor* quoted the lines in a deliberately deep voice, and he seemed to know the poem as well as she, who loved it for its rhythmic structures, and the thrill of terror that ran through the words ... words written on a dark night, perhaps, by a man gone mad from love.

They went from the hall out through another deeply cut archway into a courtyard where worn steps led down to a sunken garden of broken marble figures and a pool covered in water-lotus, whose wide leaves would harbour at night a thousand croaking frogs. Garden birds chirped in the tangle of wild vines, and the air was redolent of herbs gone to flower.

Gisela tucked her hand through the crook of Rosary's arm, for there was a sinister air about the pool and the tiled square of paving set round with urns and obelisks. Rosary noticed that Dom Duarte was gazing around him with narrowed eyes, his nostrils flared, as if he sensed the odour of a ghost!

'Long ago,' he said, 'a duel was fought here. The woman involved ran in front of her lover and received the thrust of the rapier in her heart. Here she died, by the pool, in her lover's arms.'

Rosary's eyes met the *senhor*'s in the moment that his glance flashed from the pool to her face, and she guessed instantly that a Montqueiro had been the lover. She followed his gaze to the *miradouro* attached to one of the slender towers overlooking the garden, a lady's balcony enclosed in a mesh of delicately wrought iron, a pretty cage for the girl who would have been brought all the way from Portugal to be married to a man she had probably never seen. The husband she had not loved ... and here, perhaps, she had met and found a short-lived happiness with the man she had died for.

'What happened, *senhor*?' She had to know the end of the story, for now she could feel the presence of the ghost who lingered in this garden; she saw the water-lotus stir and spin as if fingers touched them and a lizard which had been lying so still it might have been a green stone suddenly leapt high into a tangled bush of red camellia.

'For a long time the Montqueiros were banished from the island,' he said, 'until its economy began to slump. We make shrewd Governors, but we are not always wise in matters of the emotions. And now if you two girls have seen enough we will go and have lunch.'

'I've loved it here,' said Rosary impulsively. 'The old *palacio* teems with history, but I don't think you encourage tourism, do you?'

He shook his head emphatically. 'There is now plenty of work for the islanders, the farms, the fruit groves and the sea provide our food, and there are also the vineyards, the cork forest that was planted in my grandfather's time and the pottery works. We like to be self-supporting, and tourism would rob us of our individual way of life. Encourage profiteering, and those ugly hotels that spoil the coast of Portugal itself? No, *senhorita*! While I remain Governor of Vozes do Mar there will not be an influx of brash visitors from other countries. Besides, our largest beach is the Bahia de Roches, and its waters can be dangerous, and the rocks are there to protect what sand is left. My own beach is a private one.'

As he shot these words over his shoulder, he led the two girls out to the forecourt where his car waited. He told the chauffeur where to drive them. He seemed now to be withdrawn in manner, as if he regretted letting Rosary, a stranger from another country, into a dramatic secret connected with the Montqueiro fam-

124

ily. It was strange how much of the past haunted these people in whose blood ran mixed passions and the *saudade* that found a certain pleasure in sad love.

She, being young and thoughtless at times in her youth, had broken into his mood of almost enjoyable melancholy with her talk of tourism. Of course, the island must remain untouched. Its beauty lay in its isolation from the commercial race. She understood this, yet once again she had been driven to express a view which would antagonize him.

Her gaze dwelt on his hand, clenched over the handle of his stick, lean-fingered and expressing in equal measure a strength and grace and a certain violence held in check. She had angered him, and she had vowed only to disarm him.

How early, she thought, must begin the training of the Latin girl in finding her way among the twists and turns of the complex nature of the Latin male. Never in Lola's company had she ever seen him anything but relaxed and gently amused. Lola did not jolt him with the forthright questions of a British girl. She knew in her shapely bones the art of flattering with lace fan and velvety eyes. A wry smile twisted Rosary's lips. She couldn't picture herself flirting from behind a fan with this man, or ever feeling the touch of his hand in tenderness.

This thought startled her and she turned at once to Gisela and spoke at random of the dolls and jewels they had looked at and admired during their visit to the museum.

'I loved the collar of topaz,' said Gisela, putting to her nose the little flower of balsam she had plucked. 'They seemed to me exactly the colour of your eyes. Father, *minho*, do you not think that Rosary has eyes the colour of topaz?'

Rosary felt herself flush and she prayed he wouldn't answer, for his answer would surely hold a sardonic jeer only she would be aware of. Her prayer was answered, for in that instant the car turned into the parking space beside a large café, its canopied tables set out on a plaza with a view of the sea. Quite a number of people were already lunching at the tables, and heads turned and eyes followed the large grey car with the small flag of the Governor on the bonnet, and the crest of caravel and hawk on the door.

The head waiter led them to their table, with the proprietor in smiling attendance at Dom Duarte's side. Rosary felt the eyes of women diners studying her figure and her casual clothes, taking in her hair that was uncovered and very fair in the sunlight; shocked, no doubt, that she should accompany the Governor in such informal attire. When they took their seats she was aware of him bowing his dark head courteously in the direction of these women and their escorts. She saw the fine Latin teeth flash at him, and the fine eyes ... the *senhor duque*, the man in command, attractive and most eligible in the eyes of those seeking marriage for themselves, or with a daughter they would be overjoyed to have him notice.

He seemed with a flick of his eyes to notice everyone, but not by a movement of a facial muscle did he betray his awareness of what lay slumbering in the glances directed at him. He was supremely self-assured, aloof as the distant mountain peaks ... the perfect aristocrat lunching with his only child and her companion.

'What would you like to drink, Miss Bell?' he asked. 'Gisela is fond of passion-fruit juice, so perhaps you would like the same?'

'Mmm, please, *senhor*, with ice.'

He gave the order for their drinks and something rather more potent for himself. Menus were handed around the table, a large and satisfactory shield against the quizzing eyes, behind which Rosary took refuge and studied the deliciously named soups, the main courses, and the desserts steeped in the syrups and sauces made from the tropical fruits of the island.

Suddenly her sense of humour banished that slight embarrassment since Gisela's comment on the colour of her eyes. 'The menu itself is eatable,' she laughed.

'You have an appetite?' he queried. 'Shall I request that the *hors d'oeuvres* trolley be wheeled to our table?' And before she could answer him he was snapping his fingers and the trolley was being whisked to them, its white cloth laden with dishes of grilled sardine, smoked ham and salmon, slices of egg, stuffed olives, giant shrimps and baby oysters.

'Take your choice.' He obligingly held a plate while she did so, and knew him to be amused as she took an assortment of everything.

'It all looks so delicious,' she said, adding mayonnaise to the side of her plate. 'And your island air seems to give me an enormous appetite.'

'The island is not mine,' he drawled. 'I am merely the keeper of the keys. And now, Gisela, are you going to follow the example of Miss Bell and have a helping of all these good things?'

'Sim—and I do wish you would call her Rosary. When you call her Miss Bell it sounds so formal, and as if she were quite old.' Gisela grinned at him, pulled a face at the oysters and heaped her plate with the sardines, plump and silver and gleaming with oil. 'Did you notice how everyone looked at us when we arrived? How hot I'd feel in a dark suit and a hat and high-heeled shoes! Like Rosary I am always going to be casual. It's much nicer. The food and the sunshine are so much more enjoyable when one isn't formal.'

'When you grow up, child, you may wish to be exactly like other Portuguese young women.' A waiter had brought *paté* for the *senhor*, with fine pieces of golden toast wrapped in a napkin, and a small pot of butter. 'As birds are led by instinct on journeys that would kill a man, we are led by the age-old patterns in our natures. What is natural for the Senhorita Bell is not always correct for others. If the *senhoras* at the nearby tables were clad as she, with the hair in a slight disarray, they would look untidy rather than casual. The Latin has in his and her personality a certain natural formality, something connected with the features, the bearing and the attitude of mind.'

'All of which,' Gisela informed Rosary, 'means that when I grow up I shall be expected to conform to the correct pattern of behaviour. Don't you consider that I have a strict parent?'

Rosary glanced at him as he ate *paté* on toast and drank from his glass of wine, and surprisingly enough she agreed with everything he had said.

An Englishman could get away with a sports shirt and an open collar, and look ready for cricket on the green, or some punting on the river. But if a Latin male opened his collar and discarded his jacket he looked as sensuous as the devil! It was the colour of his skin that gave him a warm look, combined with the thick darkness of his hair, and often he wore a medallion on a chain about his neck, placed there when he was a young boy and unremoved for the rest of his life. Sometimes it was a crucifix meshed in the dark hair of his chest ... utterly pagan in the eyes of a woman!

A great deal of difference did exist between the Anglo-Saxon and the Latin, and being among these people had become for Rosary a voyage of discovery. She realized how much she was enjoying herself! It was a novelty to be so different from the other women at the café tables, and though at first she had felt shy of looking around at the other people, now she did so and met several pairs of very dark eyes, obviously curious about her ... especially in relationship to Dom Duarte.

There was a woman with silvery hair crowned by a toque of shining dark feathers, and when she raised her eye-glasses to study the English girl, Rosary dared to give her a smile. Immediately in response the handsome head inclined towards her, and Rosary felt as pleased as a puppy patted on the rump. The woman was undoubtedly a personage, who seemed to dominate the young men and women who lunched with her. Perhaps they were the sons and daughters of the matriarch?

'That is the Marquesa del Ronda and her family,' said Dom Duarte, whose observant eyes missed very little of what went on around him. 'She is visiting her sons from Portugal; they are the owners of the largest vineyards, and you will be meeting them when they give the annual *festa* to celebrate the fame of their wine. It is always a lively affair, and this year, Gisela, you will be old enough to attend, and to wear a long dress. There will no doubt be visitors from Portugal and it will be exciting for you.'

On their way out of the café the Marquesa and her family paused beside the *senhor*'s table in order to exchange a few words with him. He arose and kissed the old lady's hand, and she gazed up at his face before turning to smile graciously at his daughter, 'You have grown, child, since last I saw you.' Then the shrewd eyes were fixed upon Rosary. 'You have remarkably bright hair, *senhorita*. Is it natural?'

'Certainly.' Although Rosary answered smartly, she wasn't annoyed by the question. She knew from her years with Cibby that the elderly considered it their privilege to be as frank as they pleased.

'You had best beware, Duarte.' The Marquesa looked tiny but indomitable as she gazed up at him. 'I recall that your grandmother on your father's side was very fair. She came from Austria, did she not?'

'By way of the Viennese ballet, Marquesa.' He spoke blandly and looked perfectly unruffled by the implication in her words. 'She danced her way into his heart, and as I am sure you remember there was a scandal when he married her in opposition to his family's wishes.'

'You Montqueiros,' she tapped his hand with her glove, 'were always attractive and never quite predictable. You must marry again, Duarte, and still the tongues that wag about you. You must realize that you cannot remain solitary and without a son to follow you. There has never yet been a Montqueiro who has failed to pass on his name, his looks and his dash of the devil. See to it, Duarte! Perhaps before the *festa* so that you may introduce us to the fortunate young lady.'

'Marquesa,' his smile was faintly sardonic, 'you are almost the only woman I know who dares to say outright whatever is in her mind.'

'And who,' she demanded jealously, 'is this other pert creature? I say pert in her case, but I am an old friend who saw you baptized and who has watched you at play in your bath.'

He laughed, a resonant sound that rang above the clatter of cutlery and conversation. Something almost boyish in it that made Rosary blink her eyelashes ...

130

the laugh and the image of him in his baby bath were almost too much for her, and she quickly took up her wine glass in case he caught her staring at him in amazement. Yet why be amazed? He had not been born a fully grown man with a disconcerting amount of authority ... and the most unexpected charm.

'You must allow me at least one secret,' he said to the Marquesa, and once again he bent his dark head and kissed her tiny ungloved hand. Laughing a little, she went on her way, followed by her well-groomed sons and their pretty but rather subdued wives.

Rosary followed the group with her eyes, and she decided that the little Marquesa would be somewhat intimidating if one were in close contact with her. That was the risk which Latin girls took when they married a man whose mother was the head of the family.

'It must be a relief for Loreta and Mira when the Marquesa returns to her *quinta* in Portugal,' said Gisela. 'They are so much gayer when she is not here on a visit.'

'She was very beautiful,' said Dom Duarte. 'Such women do not surrender to age or youth, and they possess an armoury of wit and self-assurance gained from their many years of captivating men. Loreta and Mira must stand up to her and look her in the eye— just as our Miss Bell did.' He quirked an eyebrow at Rosary. 'I am pleased you did not permit her to annoy you, but I saw your chin take its fighting tilt.'

'Why not, *senhor*, in defence of something of my own which is not artificial. I suppose by comparison to your raven-haired women I am an oddity.'

'My child, they are not my women,' he drawled.

'They would like to be——' The words leapt impetuously from her lips, and she flushed at the way he

looked at her, half mockingly, with a hint of specula-
tion.

'People are always saying you should marry
again,' said Gisela, with a note of jealousy in her voice.
'Why don't they mind their own business? They must
know that you could never find anyone to compare
with my mother. They must realize that your heart is
buried with her.'

Rosary's heart beat with a strange quickness when
Gisela said these things, and his reply seemed as if it
would never come. She knew of the guilt he felt in
relation to Isabela, but was it really true that he had
loved her so much that remarriage was out of the question? Yet it was true what the Marquesa had said, he
had an historical name to pass on; he had estates,
pride, a shrewd governing brain. He had a young
daughter who should have a mother before she became
too possessive of her father.

'The heart dictates and duty directs,' he said carefully. 'Who can tell, Gisela, what I may feel one day
about this matter of an heir? You are old enough,
child, to understand my dilemma and my duty. I
cannot make you my heir, but I can love you very
dearly.'

Gisela's head was bent over her plate and she
wouldn't look at him. He was all she had, and Rosary
knew how much she adored him. It would wrench her
young heart in two if he should ever take another wife,
and Rosary felt sure he would wait until Gisela was a
little older, more understanding of the demands and
urges of adult life. In a year or two he would still be
an extremely virile man, and Gisela would be seven-
teen and a young woman, perhaps by then in love and
betrothed herself.

'We are all in our various ways *almas captivas*.' He

reached across and squeezed Gisela's hand, and the gleam of antique silver at his cuff caught the light and seemed symbolic of the steely pride welded into the Latin backbone, the centuries of arranged alliances which led, inevitably, to a secret gnawing hunger for love rather than a fulfilment of that hunger.

'And what,' he asked Rosary, 'holds your soul in captivity?'

'This gorgeous sweet,' she said lightly, indicating the golden fritters smothered in strawberry syrup on her plate. 'Now I know why the ladies of the harem grew so plump in their captivity.'

'Such a fate would have been beyond your bearing, I think,' he said, a deep gleam of amusement in his eyes. 'You were meant always to be a free-spirited Anglo-Saxon ... a child of nature.'

She kept thinking of those words as the car took the coast road and they followed the sea, the beckoning glitter and the blue beauty of it all. Below the road she could see the jutting rocks, cascading with green seaweed. Yes, how true it was that she responded to natural sights and sounds; they were the music of life, but something else was the substance, the intangible thing called love, the invisible and potent power that all at once took shape in the form of another human being.

She stared at the sea as the car sped homeward to the *palacete*, and all down her arm, all down the side near to Dom Duarte but not touching him, she seemed to tingle as if electricity were alive within those few inches of space.

The feeling, the awareness was rather terrible ... she had never been bodily aware of a man before, and so suddenly acute was the sensitivity of her skin that when he abruptly moved the position of his injured leg, the fine hairs at the nape of her neck seemed to creep with the abrupt fear that he had been about to touch her. It was minutes before she could relax, and when they drove into the courtyard of the palace she was out of the car before the chauffeur could open the door, leaving Dom Duarte to follow with Gisela.

In the hall she saw the Senhora de Ardo emerging from her *sala* with a friend, and they both nodded coolly as she greeted them and hurried on her way upstairs.

She had to be alone in order to sort out her confusing thoughts, and glancing swiftly downwards she saw the *senhor* engaged in conversation with the two women, while Gisela had picked up her kitten and was fondling him. Rosary hurried on and upon reaching her suite she entered and closed the door behind her with a feeling close to the relief of having eluded a pursuer.

She stood breathlessly with her back to the door, aware of the quick beating of her heart, of an emotional turmoil never felt before.

No ... this couldn't be happening to her, what she had seen happen to other girls. Student friends who developed long spells of silence while a troubling magic shimmered in their eyes. Or they became unbearably gay, as if the world could not contain their bubbling joy.

Rosary felt bewildered ... she had not a thing in common with the man, and she knew there were times when he found her about as appealing as a pain in the neck. Oh, heavens, how was she going to face him again when the very thought of his arrogant looks and his lean grace of body made her feel such a confusion of the nerves ... it was like music played discordantly when she longed for it to be played dreamily.

She ran distracted hands to her hair and walked slowly to the dressing-table, where she stood and stared at her face in the mirror, as if half fearful of seeing her secret written plainly on her features. The face that gazed back at her was shocked, but apart from that she looked much the same. She had always thought her eyes too large, her nose too small, and her mouth too wide. She thought of Lola Cortez, whose face was a perfect oval set with regular features and dusky Latin eyes.

A rueful smile curved on Rosary's lips. What a trick her own emotions had played on her! Dom Duarte endured her for Gisela's sake, and was somewhat amused by her independent antics ... thank goodness he had been unaware of her startling awareness of him in the car! That distinct fear, half desire, that he let his arm travel around her!

In the days that followed she avoided being a moment alone with him. He had work to catch up on, so it was only in the evenings, at dinner, that she saw him. At the end of the meal he would excuse himself and go to his study, or he would leave the house to call on someone. He was polite to the edge of coolness, and it was a relief, and at the same time rather unbearable to be treated to an aloof smile, or a brief question regarding Gisela's progress as a pupil.

She was growing up, learning what it felt like to be at the mercy of her emotions. She was scornful of these emotions and told herself she was reacting like some meek and lonely governess in a novel, ready to become attracted to her domineering master because there was no one in her life to care about her.

Rosary reminded herself that she had Cibby, to whom she could run for protection whenever the need arose. There was Erick, who had shown very plainly that he was attracted to her. She really had no need to be so foolish as to feel an acceleration of the pulses whenever she heard a deep Latin voice giving orders about the *palacete*; nor should she feel this craving to run like a hare whenever she caught the sound of his slight limp. He had discarded his stick, but the limp persisted to remind her that she had said an outrageous thing which he would never forgive.

It was now high summer and to avoid the heat of the afternoon she took to the woods and wandered there beneath the cool and scented shade of the pine trees and the gnarled old corks that must long ago have taken root from seed dropped from the pockets of the Portuguese sailors who had come ashore with the Montqueiro who had discovered and named Vozes do Mar. It was a name like music, and as she took aimlessly the twisting paths through the woods, with the thick shade of the trees holding at bay the hot blue dazzle of the sky, she found a certain pleasure in being alone with her disturbing thoughts.

She knew that certain of these paths led to the villa in which Lola lived with her brother, so it was no great surprise that one afternoon she should meet Lola, out with a small basket and clipping from the forks of the trees the tiny orchids that grew wild in the woods. She looked cool and lovely as a flower herself in a dark pink dress, with her hair drawn back from her face and folded into a double knot.

They did not immediately greet each other and seemed to be assessing clothes, mood, their motives for being here ... it was as if quite suddenly a sort of enmity had replaced their former cordiality. Rosary became a little embarrassed by the silence and she plunged her hands into the pockets of her pants and assumed a nonchalant air. 'It's something I can't get over,' she said, 'seeing orchids growing wild like this. Fancy being able to decorate the home with them.'

'Would you like to return to the villa with me for a cool drink?' Lola asked, and her glance as it passed over Rosary might have been lazy but for the brilliance of her pupils. 'You have never been to the villa and it is really quite nice if rather small. Duarte always tells me that I have the Latin woman's gift for making her home her world.'

Her casual and yet deliberate use of his first name went through Rosary like a small arrow. It emphasized more than anything else that Lola was a friend of his and not an employee; it implied a companionship such as Rosary would never know. The tender word, the exciting undertone, the promise of things to come.

'I——' Rosary was almost at the point of refusing Lola's invitation when she realized that she mustn't appear to be the slightest bit envious. 'I should love a cool drink. Thank you for asking me.'

'We go this way.' They continued along the path until they came to an ornamental gate in a wall. Lola opened it and they entered the garden of the villa, a gem of formality, with rose-hung pergolas, neatly tiled benches and well-kept fuchsia hedges. Not a petal or a speck of dirt lay on the paved paths to the veranda, shaded by a striped awning. There beneath the shade were rattan chairs with jewel-coloured cushions, and a circular rattan table. Nothing seemed disturbed or out of place, and Rosary thought irresistibly that it was like a picture in a glossy magazine.

The villa itself was as pretty as paint, with its curly tiles, curly iron grilles around the windows, and its tubs of well-trained plants beside the long windows leading into the house.

'Take a chair,' said Lola, 'and I will fetch the fruit

juice from the cooler. Would you like some biscuits also?'

'No, thanks. A long cool drink is all I want.'

'Are you quite certain that is all you want?' Lola gave Rosary a long cool look, and she seemed to infuse her words with a double meaning. Rosary felt the jolting of her pulse and she wondered if the Latin girl sensed in her an emotional awareness of the man who must often have sat on this veranda ... right here, perhaps, his long legs stretched across the pale pink tiling.

'The heat makes me thirsty,' she said, looking about her casually. 'You have a well ordered garden, Lola. Do you manage it yourself?'

'Yes. It is only small and passes the time for me ... until I am married. Then I shall be too occupied in other ways to be able to manage a garden.' Lola gave a soft laugh, and then with a scarlet orchid held to her lips, as if in self-reproach at giving away a secret, she walked into the house and left Rosary alone to mull over her significant words.

Rosary stared at the sun that turned to falling diamonds the water of the fountain in the centre of the garden, and it was amazing how unsurprised she was.

Lola would make an ideal wife for Dom Duarte. She would revel in his position, and his title, and enjoy every moment of being the mistress of the small palace that was enormous compared to the villa, which she obviously found a little too confining. She would be the envy of every woman on the island ... but Rosary herself felt no semblance of envy. She felt numb, after the first quick dart of pain.

# CHAPTER EIGHT

WHEN Lola returned carrying a tray of refreshments, Rosary was seated in a rattan chair, her fair head at rest against a deep gold cushion. 'How tucked away and peaceful the villa is,' she said.

'Dacio finds it a little too peaceful.' Lola smiled as she poured their drinks. 'I am quite certain he will return to Lisbon when I am no longer his responsibility. Are you sure you will not try a biscuit? I made them myself.'

'Then I will have one.' The iced morsel was delicious and Rosary took another. 'I'm afraid I can't cook anything more ambitious than bacon and eggs.'

'Instead you play music, and you do it extremely well.' Lola sat back in her chair, her silken legs gracefully crossed to reveal her fine-boned ankles. 'It will be nice for Gisela to be able to play, but of course she will never possess your skill. Do you plan a career as a music teacher?'

'It would be interesting——' Rosary tinkled the ice in her glass of lime juice. 'I do get satisfaction out of imparting what I have learned to other people.'

'But of course you will want to marry.' Lola's gaze dwelt on the English girl while her fingers played with the golden bracelet on her left wrist. 'Tell me, do you find Portuguese men attractive?'

'It would be foolish of me to say no.' Rosary smiled slightly, for how could she help but know that Lola had a specific person in mind? 'I think most Latin people are good-looking; a combination of fine eyes and very good bone structure, not to mention the raven hair. As a lover of music I suppose I'm attuned to physical beauty.'

'Our men are great charmers—some can even cast a spell over a woman.' Lola's fingers now caressed the glass her hands were holding. 'Duarte has such fascination, don't you agree? His eyes have a magnetism that might make it impossible for a woman to refuse him whatever he asked of her ... I know how much he might demand, or sacrifice, for Gisela's sake. It would be a pity for you if he demanded that you remain her companion until she is grown up. You should escape now, before he steals away your youth, that appealing freshness you have. Duarte is a ruthless man when it comes to having his own way.'

'I expect it's true to say that most men like their own way,' Rosary murmured. 'I like this island, and I have grown fond of Gisela. No one is forcing me to stay here. I have enough will of my own not to allow that.'

'Yet today in the woods you seemed a little unhappy.' Lola's gaze was velvety dark and curious. 'We are friends. You can tell me what is troubling you, if you wish to do so. Perhaps the Senhora de Ardo has been unkind again?'

'No. I think Dom Duarte has convinced her that being English I can't be expected to behave like a Latin *duena*. No, I'm not unhappy. Why should I be?' Rosary gave the Latin girl a frank look, for not by the shadow of an eyelash would she reveal to anyone the source of her slight melancholy. Everyone had to go through an attack of infatuation at some time in their life, and she would recover soon enough, and would most certainly leave the island if Lola's marriage looked like taking place before she recovered her senses. She couldn't imagine sharing a house with the bride of Montqueiro!

'When one is young——' Lola shrugged her slim graceful shoulders. 'The heart is vulnerable, and our nights are starry. It did cross my mind that you might have—well, allowed yourself to be kissed—or not kissed?'

'How very Machiavellian is the Latin mind,' Rosary smiled, and she decided to be a little cunning herself. 'Are you afraid I may have been led up the garden by your handsome brother? I must confess that I find him charming, but we are both employed at the *palacete* and we abide by the *senhora's* rules since she found us laughing together.'

'I see.' Lola swung a slim, sandalled foot, as if relaxation would not be truly hers until the act of marriage made Dom Duarte hers; and she must know that he would make her wait rather than risk making Gisela unhappy. 'Dacio is my brother and I am so accustomed to him that I forget he is not the brother of other girls. It was very daring of you to swim alone at night with him.'

'He was the perfect gentleman.'

'I am glad for your sake.'

'I am glad for my own.' Rosary stretched her arms and rose to her feet. 'Siesta will soon be over and I must be getting back to my duties. In the first cool of the evening Gisela and I practise at the piano. The keys grow so sticky during the daytime.'

'Do you find our climate at all enervating?' Lola's smooth olive skin looked cool against the filmy material of her pink dress, and not a glossy hair of her neat head was out of place. 'I have heard that very fair-skinned people feel the heat.'

Rosary stood beneath the shade of the veranda, hands at a boyish angle in the pockets of her pale tangerine slacks, and slightly amused by her own lack of poise in contrast to Lola's. She recalled what Dom Duarte had said about the great difference between the Anglo-Saxon and the Latin ... and it was like the contrast between the camellia and the daisy, which grew where it willed, running wild among the green grasses. But the camellia had to be nurtured and cared for, and kept within the boundaries of white walls and sculptured archways.

She let her smile have its way, and it was tinged with a little irony. 'Mad dogs and English girls go out in the sun regardless,' she said. 'We are a restless nation and have no gift for looking ornamental. Thank you for the cool drink, Lola, and the little chat. I gather one of the Marquesa's sons is giving a sucking-pig party on Saturday evening; a sort of *festa* to which we are all invited. I shall see you there?'

'But of course.' Lola's gaze slipped over Rosary. 'If you have not a party dress to wear, then perhaps I can lend you one of mine? We are both on the slender side——'

'No—it's kind of you, but I am only the tutor and not expected to look too glamorous.' The very idea of wearing a dress of Lola's, in which Dom Durate may have seen her, was objectionable to Rosary. As if the future mistress offered the employee a discarded garment!

'*Ate a vista.*' She sped away, running through the garden to the gate that led into the woods. She told herself that Lola had meant only to be kind, but there had been a hint of condescension in the offer which made her cheeks tingle. And aroused her battling spirit! Tomorrow she would go into the township, to the Avenida Rey, and buy the prettiest dress she could afford. On Friday evening she would wash her hair in lemon shampoo, and at the party she would be as gay and stunning as she could be.

She came out of the woods into the fading gold of the afternoon. She could see below the grounds of the *palacete* the gilded scrolls of the sea, and she heard the cries of the seabirds as the welcoming breeze blew over the land.

She loved the turn of the day, which seemed to hold elements of the dramatic, the mysterious and the subtle. Night whispered just around the corner, preparing to clothe herself in dark velvet and diamonds, and the scents of a hundred flowers. The party on Saturday would be her first real *festa*; she had missed seeing the wedding which Dacio had promised her, and she was no longer sorry. She didn't want to know any more what a Latin wedding was like; it would be too evocative of the ceremony that would one day take place between Dom Duarte and the girl she had left dreaming on a quiet veranda. The girl who wore on her wrist the golden bracelet of Latin betrothal.

Restless, seeking an outlet for her mixed emotions, Rosary walked across the courtyard and in through the windows of the room in which she studied with Gisela. She walked to the small piano and sat down at the keyboard and she began to play ... the sun had died away and the room was filled with shadows when she became aware of the tang of cigar smoke and her fingers were arrested on the keys.

'Don't stop.' The deep voice came from behind her, near the window. 'Play to the end.'

'It is ended ... almost,' she said, and she sat still in the gloom and felt the music and her dismay tingling through her body. How long had he been there, listening as she poured her secret out through her fingertips into the passionate, lyrical notes of the song composed by Liszt? Did he know the song? Would he

143

interpret her rendition as an expression of her personal feelings? She didn't dare to look at him. She didn't dare to find out.

'You must love that song very much,' he said, and his cigar smoke came drifting to her, brushing her senses almost like a touch. 'You played it, *pequena,* from the heart ... and I was here to listen instead of the young man for whom it was meant. Such a pity.'

'It wasn't meant for anyone,' she said. 'I merely felt like playing some Liszt. I—I hope you found it enjoyable——?'

'"Eternity in your arms,"' he murmured, and he came forward into the room until she felt his height and his darkness right behind her. 'Do you really expect me to believe that you were not thinking of a man during that intense performance?'

'I am sure you take it for granted that women spend most of their time thinking about men,' she rejoined. 'My grandfather taught me the song.'

'You are being evasive, *senhorita.*'

'And you are being inquisitive, *senhor.*'

He gave a soft, slightly dangerous laugh above her head, and all the time the shadows grew denser and the scents of the garden were wafted into the room by that blessed breeze. Rosary longed to leap to her feet and to rush away into the dark garden, but she knew instinctively that he was tensed for that very action.

'It's dark—I hadn't realized how the time was passing. I should get washed and dressed for dinner——'

'Stay as you are.' His hand rested briefly on her shoulder. 'My aunt has taken Gisela to the home of her friend for the evening. We are alone and will dine together in a while. Relax after your *tour de force.*'

'But'—she swung round on the stool and in the gloom she saw the glint of his eyes—'I had no idea

Gisela was going out tonight!'

'It was a sudden decision. This friend of the *senhora*'s has teenage nieces and it will be good for Gisela to be with them.'

'I see.' Rosary tensed. 'Are you becoming afraid that your daughter is having a little too much of my company? There is a remedy for that; my six weeks' trial is at an end next week.'

'Do stop leaping to conclusions.' He laughed lazily and strolled to a table on which stood a lamp. He clicked the switch and light pooled him, leaving Rosary in shadow by the piano. He wore a dark velvet smoking jacket and as he bent to stub his cigar, the definition of his profile was outlined against the silken shade of the lamp. It had a strong masculine beauty that almost made her cry out from the thrill of wonder and pain that ran through her. He straightened and she watched the movement of his lean hand over his thick black hair, and she wanted her own hand to follow the same route, wending its way down his lean cheek to his throat, his hard-boned shoulder, to his heart that was given or promised to a girl of his own race and his own instincts.

The intrusive thought of Lola brought Rosary to her feet. 'It will be tedious for you, *senhor*, dining alone with me. I can have a tray brought to my room——'

'You are as unflattering to me as you are to yourself,' he drawled. 'It can never be said that we have ever found each other's company dull. I, at least, find our conversational duels most entertaining; I am never certain when you are going to scratch me, and when you do scratch me I am never certain how I shall retaliate.'

'I am never certain of that, either,' she retorted. A

tiny, nervous smile pulled at her lip, for she wanted to be alone with him as much as she wanted to resist his persuasion, and his fascination. She could lock her door upstairs and refuse to join him for dinner ... but oh, how she would regret afterwards her denial of his subtle, charming, nerve-shattering company. His appeal to her senses (which dispelled all sensible reasoning) had become compelling; a combination of physical harmony and mental alertness.

Lola had warned her that he was hard to resist ... he was impossible to resist.

'I—I can't dine in trousers.' She backed to the door. 'I must go and put on a dress.'

He shot a glance at his wristwatch. 'I give you exactly half an hour in which to make yourself presentable.' He bowed his head with a slightly mocking formality, and she flew like a wild young bird across the hall and up the stairs, feeling as if a velvety paw had lifted a moment to let her escape. She shivered to herself as she made her way along the gallery, which felt cool and empty and seemed to underline the absence of the *senhora* and Gisela. How terribly easy it was to say of girls in love that they should have more sense of restraint than to give in to their feelings. There was a glory, and a terror, in giving in to Dom Duarte ... even to dine with such a man was an excitement out of the ordinary.

Rosary closed her door behind her, but she didn't lock it. His marriage to the lovely Lola would lock out all other women, soon enough.

With only half an hour at her disposal she swiftly showered, sprayed cool cologne from her throat to her ankles and slid into brief lingerie. She then studied her wardrobe and decided to wear a sleeveless dress made of several panels of vari-coloured chiffon, with a narrow mother-of-pearl belt. It was a youthful, unsophisticated dress, and after combing her hair she let it curve on her shoulders, and she applied to her lips some pale, shining pink colour.

She studied herself in the mirror and for a panicky moment she wondered if she looked too showy ... she had last worn this dress at a student dance, and she certainly didn't wish to give the impression that she was expecting dinner with the Dom to be a party affair.

In the silence she heard the striking of the clock that stood on the gallery, antique and demanding, warning her that she had no more time to waste on her appearance. Snatching up a chiffon handkerchief, she walked from her suite ... when she reached the stairs her fingers clenched on the chiffon, for he was down in the hall, by the door that led to and from the wine cellars. She made no sound as she stood there, bracing herself to go down, and he turned as if his senses were always on the alert and he glanced up at her and his eyes, passing swiftly over her, disturbed her nerves and her emotions more than ever. He seemed not to miss a detail of her dress, her bare arms, and slim legs in sheer nylons. Then he was looking at her hair, loose and silvery about her young face that sought so frantically to look cool and composed.

He came to the foot of the stairs and he carried a long-necked bottle in his hand. 'You look the spirit of youth,' he said. 'Perhaps I should offer you fruit juice instead of wine?'

She stood with a slim foot poised on the stairs, knowing she must descend or retreat to her room. Tiger-eyes sparkled in the lobes of her ears; the little jewelled earrings which had belonged to her mother. With a sudden little gesture of bravado Rosary tossed

147

her head, making them sparkle all the more as she went down to him. She smiled gaily, acting the woman of the world.

'I shall be most disappointed if you don't give me wine, *senhor*,' she said. 'I'm not a child, you know.'

'No, not a child, nor yet a woman.' He continued to stand there as she drew nearer to him. 'You are at the stage when "Your slim gilt soul walks between passion and poetry." '

'Oscar Wilde!' she exclaimed, and her eyes were wide as a child's in that moment, and then her lashes were lowered with the secretiveness of a woman. 'You seem to know a lot of poetry, *senhor*.'

'The Portuguese are fond of it,' he said casually. 'Shall we go to the *sala*? I have ordered our dinner to be served there tonight. Two people at that long table in the dining-room seem like strangers before the meal is half over.'

Her heart made a soft thunder in her breast as she walked with him across the glowing tiles of the floor to the rosewood doors of the *sala*. It both frightened her, and excited her, that tonight he didn't wish to be aloof and alone at the head of the table, which even with four people seated there seemed too grand, isolating one from the other, with silver candelabra and flowers in between.

They entered the *sala*, lit by lamps, and with birds and flowers worked in silk thread on the brocade curtains and upholstery of chairs and sofas. A circular table had been laid for dinner, with two chairs facing each other.

She wanted to look at him, to question his eyes, to ask with her own eyes why it pleased him to dine like this with his daughter's tutor. Tiny flickers of alarm zigzagged through her body. She had heard tales of men of wealth, who had whims and fancies which they satisfied and then coolly dismissed from their conscience. Men who honoured the woman they meant to marry, but who thought it merely a game to seduce a girl who was foolish enough to walk like a fly into the carefully spun web.

She heard the closing of the doors behind him, and felt his silent tread across the Indian carpet that was sensuously soft under the thin soles of her evening shoes. She tautened, and wondered if he meant to explore her unawakened passions.

Rosary swung to face him and the tiger-eyes glittered against her pale, untouched skin. 'What sort of a girl do you think I am?' She blurted the words, untrained as yet in the art of being subtle.

His eyes narrowed as he looked down at her. Then he glanced at the table laid for two, at the lamps that cast small pools of gold and ruby light on to the cushioned sofas. Suddenly, wickedly, he smiled as she had never seen him smile before. 'Quite often an infuriating one,' he replied. 'Right now your agile young mind is grappling with several reasons why I should ask you to dine alone with me, and that tilt to your chin tells me that I have been cast in the role of dangerous Latin with seduction on his mind. Am I right?'

'It is always inclined to cross a girl's mind, especially when she knows——'

'Knows what?' he broke in swiftly.

'Oh, that she has nothing in common with the man and is merely a form of amusement.'

'You consider that it would merely amuse me to seduce you?' He was looking directly at her, a slightly mocking smile on his lips. 'The amusement, *pequena*, will be in holding you on tenterhooks, keeping you in suspense as to my intention ... ah, how large grow your eyes! Did you fondly imagine that once the subject was mentioned the danger would decrease? How innocent you really are! This sort of frankness between a man and a woman only increases the fun.'

'I—I think I will have that tray in my room!' Rosary went to brush past him, and with a quick movement he caught her wrist in his fingers and prevented her from leaving.

'You surprise me,' he drawled. 'I didn't take you for a coward.'

'I'm not,' she flung at him, and the indignant movement of her head set the tiger-eyes dancing in her earlobes. 'I'm not afraid of you——'

'Perhaps you are afraid of yourself?'

'Why should I be?' She defied his eyes, and her own riot of emotions as he held her so that the chiffon panels of her dress were caught like moth wings against the dark velvet of his jacket. 'Do you consider yourself so irresistible, *senhor duque*? Have you practised before your *senhor* rights on other amusing creatures like myself ... oh, don't, you'll break my wrist!' She cried out as his fingers tightened, gripped, until the bones of her wrist seemed about to snap in two. 'You are ruthless ... Lola told me you are!'

'So! You have been discussing me with Lola?' His teeth snapped whitely and his dark face came down close to Rosary's, menacing and yet still with that quality of masculine beauty that thrilled through her very bones. 'I hope it was an interesting and enlightening conversation?'

'Extremely so. I know the betrothal is not yet official, but girls like to share secrets, and I saw the bracelet on her wrist.' His closeness was making Rosary breathless ... oh, how dared he behave like this! He was playing with her like a hawk with a bird, perhaps in a reckless mood because at last he had committed himself to the marriage that everyone expected of him ... the marriage that would upset Gisela, and disturb the beautiful ghost of Isabela. He perhaps felt driven to take out on someone his doubts and his angers, but why pick on her? It was so unfair of him ... and she loved him so!

She loved him even as she hated him for being so cruel and mocking ... she almost fell as suddenly there was a tap on the door and he let go his grip on her.

The doors opened and the dinner trolley was wheeled into the room by a manservant. Rosary stared past the man into the hall ... the doors of the cage were open and she could flee this moment and Dom Duarte would not stop her in front of his servant. She was as tensed as an arrow quivering in the bow, poised to fly from him.

'Come, *senhorita*,' his voice was deep but not demanding. 'Don't let the food get cold.'

She looked at him, but now his face was an inscrutable mask, and he was holding ready her chair for her, while the manservant hovered, ready to serve them from the array of dishes on the trolley. On the table the wine stood ready, and the camellias nestled their creamy cheeks together on their bed of fern. The lace of the cloth was intricately Portuguese against the gleaming wood of the table. The lamps burned softly, and like a prisoner of a dream she walked to where he stood holding ready her chair and she slipped into it. When he took his own chair she studied his face through her lashes to see if he mocked her capitulation, but his features were as if shaped by a chisel and set in bronze, and his attention was upon the wine as he drew the cork; he tasted it and then almost filled the flute glasses.

'This was bottled and put down in my grandfather's time,' he said, when the manservant had left them, closing the doors and leaving them alone together. 'It was wine distilled from the grapevines his bride brought from Austria. Taste it.'

She did so and found it delicately sharp-sweet, like a kiss. 'It's very nice,' she said.

'It's a little more than that.' He ate a wing of pheasant and drank again from his glass. 'Did it surprise you to learn that my grandmother was a Viennese ballerina?'

Her glance skimmed his shoulders and she thought of his height, which had always surprised her in a Portuguese. 'I rather had the feeling, *senhor*, that somewhere along the line a certain element not quite Latin had crept into your ancestry. You are the tallest man on this island.'

He smiled abruptly. 'It has its advantages. Will you have some more green peas ... another wing of bird?'

'I have enough, *senhor*, thank you.'

His eyes skimmed her face. 'Your appetite is usually a hearty one. Are you still nervous of my motives in arranging this dinner for two?'

She shrugged her shoulders. 'I have committed myself to your motives, *senhor*, so I suppose I must take the consequences.'

'Ah, come,' he quirked an eyebrow, 'if you submit without a fight then you rob the game of half its appeal. More wine?'

'No—yes,' she added defiantly. 'It might help to numb my feelings, for I have already learned that to fight with you is to get bruised.'

'Bruised?' he echoed. 'Show me!'

She extended her wrist and there against the pale

skin was the mark of his fingers. 'I am not made of plastic, *senhor*. I can be hurt, you know, and it isn't fair of you to think I can be used. I'm not a member of the permissive society because I happen to work abroad far from my family ... not a very large one, consisting as it does of only my grandfather.'

'Child, do stop!' He gave a laugh that was half a groan, and suddenly he was upon his feet and striding round the table to her side. He took the hand she had extended to him and he examined the bruises he had caused. 'I am a brute, eh? A ruthless tyrant, who amuses himself at your expense. You hate me, eh?'

'Yes,' she said, and pulled her hand free of his, as if his touch was detestable rather than desirable ... and the extent of that desire of hers was truly amazing, all things considered. It made her eyes blaze up at him, for somehow, no matter how, she had to find protection from him, a shield against his devastation of her feelings.

'When I first came here you said you would be like a guardian to me, and you told me to try and behave like a Latin girl. I have tried to abide by your rules, *senhor*, but you seem tonight to be breaking your own.'

'Do I, Miss Bell?' He gazed for a long intent moment over her head, and then he inclined his own head in agreement. 'Please relax now and be serene. It is just that tonight the *palacete* is filled with a black memory which I have tried to dispel by playing the devil. Each year this happens and you are right, I have tried to use your youth and your innocence to try and hold at bay the dark phantom of memory.'

He returned to his place at the table and his face wore a brooding look as he refilled his wine glass, and looking at him she suddenly knew why he had sent

Gisela to play and talk with young people; why a sort of devil did seem in possession of him tonight.

As compassion gripped her, she no longer had any armour against him, or wanted it. 'Grief was never a reasonable emotion,' she murmured.

He glanced up from his contemplation of his wine, and held her in the deep-set, alive and searching gaze of his eyes. 'Don't call it grief,' he said. 'You were right the last time when you called it conscience. It is exactly six years to this day that my wife was killed, and all day I have been remembering how she died ... she who loved luxury and beautiful things ... shining things, like gems and the well-groomed coat of her horse. She married me to have them, and I married her, a young man bedazzled by her beauty.'

He tossed back his wine and the action had something reckless about it, and for a moment it was as if the youthful Montqueiro sat facing Rosary, his strong mouth sullen and disillusioned.

'You have been to the gallery to look at her portrait, eh?'

'Yes, *senhor*. Your wife was strikingly beautiful.'

'The artist, like all other men, was in love with her ... unlike me, who had then lived with her for seven years, they were unaware that she lacked humanity, which is an awareness of the feelings of others. Love is when the heart unlocks itself, but she kept hers for ever guarded, like the jewels I gave her. The strange, deep yearnings that are love slowly died in me, until even desire turned to stone. Can you bear to stay and hear why we quarrelled that day ... six years ago today?'

'If you wish to tell me, *senhor*.'

'I think I do wish!' He rose abruptly to his feet, towering there, still with something devilish about him in the lamplight. 'Come away from the table ... the left food and the dregs of the wine!'

He walked away, to the windows, where he stood framed by the long brocade curtains, lean hands thrust into the pockets of his black velvet jacket, a tie of dark silk against the whiteness of his shirt. Rosary went and sat on a sofa, and though apart from him, her entire being seemed to reach out to him. As she gazed at him, her arms at rest on the back of the sofa, her posture was young, but her eyes offered the understanding of Eve ... of Venus herself.

Though he denied it something of his youthful love of Isabela remained and would always remain, part of him, and part of Gisela.

'That morning at breakfast,' he said, 'she asked me to ride with her. She said she had something to discuss with me. Why deny that even then I was hopeful of something taking a turn for the better in our marriage? I don't deny it, but it was an empty hope. Gisela was then nine years old, springing up and no longer a toddler. Isabela had an almost pathological desire never to look or grow a day older, but a growing daughter reveals that the mother is a little older each month, each year. Isabela had decided that she didn't like this evidence of her maturity in front of her each day and she wished me to enrol Gisela in a boarding school in Portugal. I refused! I told Isabela in no uncertain terms that Gisela would remain at home with us until she was eleven. Time enough then to send her to school. One word led to another. We quarrelled as never before ... "You might as well know," I said, "that I intend to have a son from you as well as a daughter." Immediately she slashed at me with her riding whip, and then she tore off on the back of the horse, whipping the poor beast as she would have liked to whip me. Maddened herself, she made the animal mad, and he threw her, and as he danced with pain he kicked her and she died, still beautiful, still quite young, and hating me.'

The last words fell away into silence and he was so very still that when at last he moved the movement startled Rosary. He came slowly to where she sat and he held out his hand and after a shy, wordless pause she gave hers to a clasp that left her defenceless.

'Forgive me for hurting you,' he said, 'but now, perhaps, you understand my demon? Do you?'

'Yes, *senhor*, I think so.'

'You are not too shocked?'

'No,' she shook her head, 'only sad.'

'For Isabela?' The golden lights glimmered deep within his eyes, the embers of the love which Isabela had killed with her coldness. Looking up at him Rosary wanted to reach up to him, to pull his face close to hers and kiss away that sardonic, almost weary look.

'Sad for all three of you,' she said, and because of what she felt her hand tensed within his, and he looked at it and still with that sardonic air he bent his head and kissed her wrist.

'Yes, a child should have a mother,' he said. 'I wonder if I asked you to play once more tonight you would oblige? Something to dispel the shadows, eh?'

'If you wish, *senhor*.' She rose to her feet and her hand slipped from his, bringing close to her side the kiss that lingered on her bruised wrist. They walked together to the larger salon and he opened the grand piano for her, lit the candles and turned out the main lights.

'*Les Sylphides*,' he murmured, and his eyes flicked

her ashen hair in the candlelight. 'You know the music, of course?'

'Of course.' Her smile was shy and swift, and she was both glad and a little regretful when he retreated into the shadows to listen to the music that evoked, perhaps, a boyish memory of his grandmother, a dancer in a misty white dress, a sweet ghost that did not torment him.

Rosary played on and on for him, until suddenly, stridently, the telephone rang in the hall. He excused himself and went to answer it. When he returned his expression by the glow of the candles was unreadable. 'Aunt Azinha and Gisela have arranged to stay the night at her friend's house,' he said. 'My aunt has a fear of night-time driving, and so I have agreed to the arrangement.'

'It will make a nice change for Gisela, *senhor*.'

'Quite so.' He began to wander about the room, picking up ornaments and quizzing them, and then putting them down again. 'It has not been such a nice change for you, eh, dining with a man of unpredictable moods? Tell me, are you looking forward to the *festa* at the weekend?'

'Immensely. It will be my first real chance to listen to the *fados* and to watch the dancing.'

'Dancing and music are the pleasures of the gods.' He stood holding a little figurine and Rosary saw the glimmer of his teeth in a reflective smile. 'Love is the third pleasure, if one ever finds it. Do you miss the young man in England?'

The question sprang at her, softly and dangerously as a springing cat. *What young man?* she almost cried, and then she recalled the white lie she had told about Erick. 'Oh,' she said, 'of course.'

'How shy the British are of speaking their love,' he

mocked. 'The Liszt song was far more expressive of your feelings. How would it be if I arranged for him to fly to Vozes do Mar for the weekend, so that you might enjoy the *festa* together?'

'No——' She sprang to her feet. 'No, he wouldn't be able to get away from the orchestra. *Senhor*, please leave my personal feelings alone! I don't question yours!'

'Mine, Miss Bell?' His gaze was directly upon her through the candle glow and his height, his danger, seemed intensified.

'Yours—with regard to Senhorita Cortez.' The sudden tiredness of spent emotions swept over Rosary, making her reckless. 'I hope I proved a satisfactory stand-in for her tonight, *senhor*? Thank goodness I have not been so guarded from life as a Latin girl, otherwise I might have been shocked to learn that love can be a hurtful thing. I am sure you wouldn't want to disillusion the woman you are going to marry!'

The words rang out in the silence of the room, and then in the electric pause that followed Rosary ran to the double doors and flung them open with a sort of desperation. She expected any second to feel him breathing down her neck, and it wasn't until she was halfway across the hall, with the baroque stairway looming ahead of her, that she realized he hadn't moved. He had let her go as if too contemptuous to be angry with her. As she went upstairs she dragged her feet a little, rather like a tired adolescent going home from a party she wasn't sure she had enjoyed. She watched the pale glitter of her evening shoes against the darkness of the stairs, and felt the soft swing of chiffon against her legs. Her mood was pitched between excitement and tears, and when she reached the head of the stairs she paused to gaze at the archway that led into the picture gallery.

Suddenly she felt a compulsion to look at the face of Isabela, to see again the beauty which had bewitched Duarte.

# CHAPTER NINE

ROSARY pushed aside the velvet curtains over the archway and switched on the wall lights, so arranged to shine on the paintings. Somewhere a window was open and as she made her way along the gallery the perfume of datura wafted in from the gardens.

Montqueiro eyes seemed to follow her from the portraits, and the sound of her own footsteps was somehow intrusive, for everything was so quiet, so enshrouded by the moonless night.

The gleam of a red gown and white arms drew her to the portrait which she had last seen on Dacio's work table. Now it was hung and the colours had been so revived that the raven hair and creamy skin of Isabela were almost touchable. Her dress and her jewels gleamed richly, and her dark eyes seemed to meet and hold Rosary's. They held a subtle little smile, as if she mocked the artist who had painted her with such admiration.

The minutes passed, one after the other, as Rosary studied the flawless face, the long line of the neck encircled by gems, the hands whose fingers had that curious plumpness of greedy hands. Suddenly a cold shiver ran through her and she turned away from the portrait. It was too perfect a beauty, with a flawed soul.

Reaching the velvet-hung archway, she turned out the lights and slipped silently out of the picture gallery ... and walked unaware into a pair of arms that reached out of the dimness and closed around her, making a prisoner of her.

'So you had to go and look at her!' Dark eyes blazed down at Rosary, too stunned for the moment to move or speak. 'You had to find in her beauty the brute that I am, eh? This much a brute ... and this!'

She was swept painfully close to him, and as her head reared back so that she might speak, might let him know that she didn't condemn him for wanting a warm and giving woman, his mouth came down on hers as if he revenged himself on her.

His lips were warm and hard and scornful in their taking ... his left hand raked upwards into her hair, gripping the pale silk of it, and his right arm was cruel in its strength as it locked her to him, from her breast to her hips. Savagely, deliberately, he kissed her until in her maddened attempt to get away from him she was kicking his ankles.

'You little wildcat!' Still he gripped her hair and stared down at her white, almost desperate face, that of a girl swept for the first time into the deeps of a man's angry passion. The silence stretched, and then was broken as his arms slid away from her and the cool night air along the galley came between them, scented with datura. 'Tomorrow I shall doubtless be walking with a stick again,' he said drily.

'Oh—your ankle!' Free of him, she backed away, but into her eyes leapt instant contriteness, the memory of him pinned beneath an overturned car. 'I didn't think——'

'Nor did I.' He gave her a sardonic little bow. 'Kicks for kisses would seem appropriate in the circumstances. *Bom noite*, Miss Bell, and let me add that there will be no need for you to lock your bedroom door. A wrenched shoulder from forcing it open, and a battered ankle, would really be too much for even Casanova.'

Again with a bow, and something of amusement at the way she had fought him, he turned on his heel and walked away. She stared after his tall figure, and having known his fury she wondered, with a swift acute wonder, what his tenderness was like.

Madness ... she ran her fingers through her hair and felt her tingling scalp, and ran all the way to her room. Crazy ... to love him, and to hate him at the same time.

She leant from her balcony and breathed the pervasive scent of Angel's Trumpet. The night seemed heady with it ... her senses rocked and swam with datura, and the lingering ache of Duarte's mouth on hers.

*Cibby, what shall I do?* She pressed her cheek to the cool stonework and she hungered to be a child again, protected and directed by her grandfather's wisdom. Should she go home ... now ... next week, before it became too unbearable to see Duarte each day and to know that each week brought nearer and nearer his marriage to Lola? When she had mentioned the betrothal bracelet he had made no denial of being the donor. When he had kissed her it had been from anger, not desire.

When would he let it be known that he had decided to marry again ... at the *festa,* as the Marquesa del Ronda had suggested?

Rosary had looked forward to the *festa,* but now she had a dread of it. Was she a good enough actress to greet with a smile the official announcement of the Governor's engagement to Lola, who was so lovely, so Latin, so ready to make the perfect wife for him? Wearily she walked into her bedroom and removed her chiffon dress, the little tiger-eyes from her earlobes and the gay little slippers from her feet. She wandered

162

about her room preparing for bed, and with her ruffled silvery hair and slightly shadowed eyes she looked very young, and yet had never felt so adult before.

What would she have done had she been more a woman of the world? Would she have fought Duarte, or given in to his furious kisses? As there rushed over her again all those alarming sensations aroused by his lips on hers, she buried her face in her hands, almost as if she prayed for the strength to withstand this sudden assault on her emotions by a man who had kissed her to punish her, and who by now would have quite forgotten those wild moments on the threshold of the picture gallery.

For her it had been the threshold of discovery ... when she had kicked him, she had kicked to be free of her increasing longing never to be free of his lips, his arms, his lean and dangerous body. She plunged out the bedroom light, but couldn't erase from her mind every feature of his face ... or blot from her body a sense of need unknown until now; an aching desire to be wanted by him. She lay staring into the darkness and it was a long time before she fell asleep.

In the morning she felt more composed, but was glad when she went down to breakfast to find that he was already at work in his study, and she had the patio table to herself. She was drinking a second cup of coffee when Dacio arrived for his day's work. As he came through the arched entrance he paused to give her a rather searching look. 'All alone and just a little blue?' he asked.

'You may join me for some coffee and then I shan't be alone,' she said gaily.

He came and sat on one of the low walls that rambled around the patio, and she rang the little bell and Manoel brought another cup and saucer to the table. She poured his coffee and gave him a smile as she handed it to him. 'If the weather stays like this for the *festa*, then it will be wonderful. I am told that people are coming all the way from Portugal for the celebration. It will be very interesting for me, my first real chance to see the islanders in their traditional costumes.'

'It will certainly be an occasion for Lola.' Dacio's gaze dwelt on Rosary's face, which in the morning sunlight was paler than she realized, with still a hint of shadow about her brown eyes. With a supreme effort of will she forced herself not to look away from Dacio; compelled herself not to betray any emotion other than friendly interest.

'I saw your sister yesterday and she told me she would soon be leaving you to your own resources. Her betrothal bracelet is very beautiful.'

'Lola was always determined to marry a man who would give her the good things in life.' He plucked a small flower from the cluster that overhung the wall, put it to his lips and with a careless gallantry he tossed it to Rosary. It fell on the table by her hand, but she didn't dare to pick it up. Her hand would crush it ... she could feel in her fingers the urge to crush something. Yes, Duarte could offer all this, but surely for a second time he wasn't going to find himself bound to a woman who wanted *things*! Rosary thought of Lola at the villa yesterday, her emphasis on the fact that the place was small and she looked forward to a much grander house.

'Don't you want the flower?' Dacio murmured. 'You aren't a girl who prefers gold bracelets, are you?'

'No.' She shook her head. 'I've been eating honey and my fingers are sticky. But, Dacio, I am sure Lola is

164

terribly in love with ... him?'

He laughed softly. 'You also place love above rubies, eh?'

'I should hope so, if one is to find any real happiness in this life!'

'Do you think you could love me?' he asked, almost casually.

'Don't jest about it,' she said, and her voice shook a little, for she was learning the hard way that love was a serious matter and not a game. 'Just because Lola is soon to be married you mustn't get in a panic for another housekeeper.'

'You little *diabo*!' Immediately he was on his feet, and with a stride he was around the table, and Rosary cried out as he gripped her arms, where someone else had left bruises, and dragged her to her feet. He shook her, and then quickly bent his head and kissed her startled mouth.

'*Bom dia*.' The voice was smooth and cold as ice. 'I am about to drive into town and wondered, Miss Bell, if you have some shopping you would like to do. I am informed by telephone that Gisela is now going to a picnic, so you have a holiday.'

Rosary's feelings were impossible to describe as she edged away from Dacio ... his kiss had meant nothing, but the fact that Duarte had witnessed it was mortifying. What would he think of her? She, who had kicked his sore ankle in her desperation to escape his kisses! With Dacio she had been passive in her surprise, and also unafraid of him, but Duarte wasn't to know that. He had observed a girl submitting without a struggle to a young man's kiss, on a sunlit patio, surrounded by flowers and the music of bees.

All she could do was to accept politely his offer of a lift into town.

'I will go and fetch my handbag, *senhor*.'

'Don't run, Miss Bell. I am not going immediately.'

Her eyes brushed his face, a polite mask of lean distinction, with a hint of scorn about the lips that last night had been so close to hers. He wore a white suit, with a pale tan shirt. He looked ... oh, she didn't dare to think of how he looked. All she knew was that he belonged to someone else, and she, Rosary, was the one who cared madly for him. Yes! Madly! So that it wouldn't have mattered to her if he were a boatman rather than the Governor of the island.

He made polite and impersonal conversation as they drove along in the car which had replaced the Porsche. When they reached the Avenida Rey he didn't offer to pick her up for lunch, but said he would be waiting to drive her home at three o'clock, outside the Administration building.

'I am sure you can amuse yourself until then,' he said.

'Of course, *senhor*. I wish to buy a dress for the *festa*, and then I might have a look around the old *palacio* again.'

'You must have some lunch,' he said briskly. 'I fear I shall be tied up until this afternoon, but you are not a young woman who needs to lean upon a man, are you?'

'No, *senhor*.' For the first time that morning she met his eyes, and found them as impersonal as his face. 'I shall find a harbour café and eat lobster salad, and strawberries and cream.'

He frowned slightly, and his eyes flicked over her, taking in her bright uncovered hair, and the sleeveless dress she wore, cut halfway to her waist at the back and deliciously cool and short. 'I should prefer that you don't choose a café frequented by the fishermen,' he said curtly.

'Why, are you afraid I shall flirt with one of them?'
She spoke the words with a painful rush of feeling, for
his glance criticized her dress ... her entire person, and
it was hard to endure when she longed ... oh, for the
unattainable.

'I have warned you before,' his cutting tone of voice
made her flinch, 'that Latin men have a fire in them
that you would find hard to extinguish if you roused it
uncontrollably with your careless disregard for convention.' Suddenly he put an arm around her waist
and just about swept her into the biggest department
store on the *avenida*. His fingers snapped and a saleswoman in a sedate dark dress came running to attend
to his demands.

'I wish to buy a coat for the young lady,' he said.
'Something in a light material—tussore, perhaps!'

Rosary was overwhelmed by him, ordered not to say
a word as a selection of coats were shown to him. One
of them was silvery grey, with a high mandarin collar
and full sleeves. 'Try it on,' he said to her, and with a
mutinous set to her lips she did so. She hoped it
wouldn't fit her, but it fitted perfectly, and had that
light and glamorous feel of an expensive garment.

'That is the one,' he said decisively. 'Please to put it
on my account, and also——'

'No!' Rosary gave him a fierce look that stopped the
words on his lips. He would not pay for her dress for
the *festa*, even if he was determined to buy the coat, to
cover sedately the arms and neck of his daughter's
tutor.

'Very well.' He inclined his head. 'I should like your
promise that you will wear the coat when you leave
the shop and go and have lunch.'

'If you insist.' She forced a little laugh to her lips.

'How very conventional you Latins are—in public!'

Instantly he guessed her meaning and as she saw the tiny danger signals leap to life in his eyes she tilted her chin and dared him with a look to lose in public his well-controlled temper. She knew, as the saleswoman and the other shoppers couldn't know, that he leashed that leaping temper only seconds before he gave a brief bow and left the shop, allowing the doors to swing sharply behind him.

A momentary silence followed his departure, and then people began to speak again in low tones. Rosary felt sure they were speaking about her; she felt their glances on the tussore coat and for a moment she almost panicked and dashed through the swing doors in the wake of Duarte. He was arrogant enough not to care that people might gossip about his every action, but Rosary cared, and she turned quickly to the saleswoman. 'The *senhor* was kind enough to buy me the coat for my birthday.' She spoke so her voice carried, and after all it was only a white lie; her birthday was only a week away. 'He's very generous to the people who work for him.'

'Indeed he is, *senhorita*. Firm but never the tyrant.'

'No, never the tyrant.' Rosary smiled slightly. 'I should now like to see some evening dresses, and this time I am treating myself.'

'Has the *senhorita* a particular colour in mind?' As they walked to the lift the silk coat rustled softly and expensively, and glances of unveiled curiosity followed the English Miss with the silvery hair. She felt her cheeks warming up; it was quite a new experience for her to be thought a *femme fatale*.

The morning passed and the dress she finally decided on was an intriguing blend of white and pale green silk, very simple in design, but with a sweeping skirt that made her seem tall and willowy, and gave her a much needed sense of assurance.

Dacio had intimated that the *festa* was going to be a special occasion for Lola, which must mean that her engagement was going to be officially announced. When that moment came Rosary was going to need all the courage that her resilient youth and a pretty dress could bring to her aid. A gay smile must be her shield, and the garment of silk her armour.

After arranging to pick up her dress around three o'clock, Rosary left the shop and made her way along the palm-lined *avenida* towards the noisy, bustling market-place. Here the streets were narrow and stepped, wending their way down to the colourful harbour, where below the long cobbled sea-wall the fishing boats with their high prows were drawn up on the sands.

Rosary stood by the sea-wall and watched a picturesque old fishing boat bringing in the crab and lobster pots, alive with the clawed creatures. Peddlers of fish, cheese and golden loquats carried their wide baskets on their heads, and the clatter of wooden sandals on the cobbles mingled with the talk and laughter of people haggling around the market stalls.

She felt an eager longing to be part of all this, to have a stake in the island, an assured future among these pleasant and happy people. But it was a forlorn hope. Nothing on earth would keep her at the *palacete* when Lola became its mistress. It wasn't that she disliked the Latin girl ... it was that she loved the Governor.

'Love is a devil', she thought, and with a rueful smile she glanced at her wristwatch and realized that the lunch hour was upon her and she must find a quiet café where she could eat without feeling conspicuously alone. The smart café where she had lunched with Duarte and his daughter was out of the question. It was far too expensive, and too many of his friends lunched there.

On impulse she approached one of the *varinas* who stood resting her basket of fish on the harbour wall, the bright sleeves of her blouse bunched up around her muscular arms. '*Bom dia, amiga,*' Rosary greeted her, and went on to ask if she knew of a nearby café that was secluded and inexpensive.

The *varina* looked at her with a friendly curiosity, running her dark gaze over the sunlit hair of the *Inglesa,* studying her features that were so different from those of her swarthy self. She gestured along the harbour to where the colour-washed houses were situated. If the *senhorita* was on her own, then she would find it pleasant to eat at the *quinta.* She would locate it quite easily, for it was a whitewashed house set within a garden of fruit trees.

'You are kind.' Rosary thanked her and proceeded in the direction of the houses. Soon she came in sight of white, thickly crusted walls, and an ornamental gate leading into a garden where tables were arranged under the fruit trees. The *quinta* itself had a picturesque jumble of red-tiled roofs, casement windows and deep doorways framed in cascades of a bougainvillea.

Rosary stood entranced by the place, and pleasure was swiftly followed by a stab of regret. How she would have loved to lunch here with Dom Duarte, beneath those custard-apple trees, with their enormous leaves gold-flecked and shading the table which stood within sound of the trickling water of the irrigation wheel. She removed the coat he had bought her and hung it over the adjacent chair; it made the chair seem less bare and unoccupied.

A young waitress came to her table and with a smile of welcome she handed her a menu, from which Rosary selected ice-cold cream soup, and lobster salad to follow, with a glass of wine. She then sat breathing the scents of the garden ... how peaceful it was after the bustle of the harbour, and there were no bold young fishermen to ogle her and call out those Latin compliments that always sounded so risqué. The other tables were mainly occupied by young couples intent on each other; the girls' *duenas* appeared to be lunching together at other tables.

The waitress served her cream soup, and she seemed to look at Rosary with sympathy in her eyes. Rosary gave her a gay little smile, as if to deny that it didn't hurt, or matter, that she had no attentive Latin to look at her as if she made his sunshine.

The lobster meat was removed from the shell for her and arranged on a bed of crisp lettuce; with it were slices of tomato and cucumber, a delicious sauce, crusty bread and sweet butter. Her glass of amber-coloured wine made her feel almost carefree, and the sweet wild strawberries and cream that followed made her think of childhood holidays and roaming the Devon hills with Cibby, whose affection had been all-sufficing until she came to Vozes do Mar and discovered another kind of love.

After lunch she roamed the *quinta* gardens instead of going to the museum, and discovered a little domed gazebo set round with great ferns that drooped against its walls, with blue passion-flowers climbing its roof. She was about to enter when she caught the murmur of a male voice and the soft laughter of a woman. She quickly retreated and told herself ruefully that the *quinta* was a place for lovers and she was an intruder

... anyway, it must be almost three o'clock, for she had dallied over her lunch, and she ought to be getting back to the shop to pick up her dress.

She glanced at her wristwatch and saw that the hands stood at two-thirty. Ample time for her to stroll back to the shop and meet the car outside the Administration building.

A slumbrous siesta quiet lay over the town, and the harbour looked so deserted that it was unbelievable it had been so busy a couple of hours ago. On the beach some fishermen lay sleeping in the shade of their boats, and the sun and the sea had merged into a dazzling glow. The palm trees along the Avenida Rey were as becalmed as everything else, their fans spread green and still against the blue sky. She arrived at the shop and entered through the swing doors. She went up in the lift to the dress department, where to her relief she found a girl crouched at the feet of a display model, busily stitching the hem of a white satin gown.

Rosary explained that she had come to fetch a dress she had bought that morning. It was already wrapped and labelled for her. The girl nodded and went to fetch it, and Rosary stood looking at the lovely white gown on the display model. It had long tight sleeves with crystalled cuffs, a high neck with a crystalled collar and a long full skirt with a train. It was quite stunning, and quite obviously a wedding gown.

When the girl returned with Rosary's dress box, and knelt again to continue with her stitching, it seemed the most natural thing to ask who the lucky bride was to be. The girl glanced up with a smile. 'The material was sent from Portugal, *senhorita*. The dress has been specially made for the marriage of the Senhorita Cortez ... she will make a lovely bride, I think.'

'She will indeed,' said Rosary, and she said *adeus*

and felt curiously numb as she left the department store, as if the pain would be too hard to endure if she gave in to it. She walked back along the *avenida* without noticing the heat or the stillness, and when she came in sight of the Administration building she pinned a smile to her lips and was determined to look as if she had enjoyed every moment of her shopping, and her lonely lunch in a garden made for lovers.

She saw the bronze-coloured car standing at the kerb of the paved entrance to the handsome building, with its façade of gorgeous *azulejos*, and stone lions guarding the steps. The only sound as she made her way to the car was that of the water falling into the marble basins of the fountain that stood in the forecourt, splashing down over the mermaids and the huge conch shells. A long shadow slanted in the sunlight, and Rosary's heart beat fast as Dom Duarte came unhurriedly towards her.

'I—I hope I haven't kept you waiting,' she said, 'I had to return to the shop to collect my dress.'

'Ah yes, the intriguing dress for the *festa*.' His eyes smiled a little as he took the box and put it on the back seat of his car. 'You had a good lunch, I hope?'

'Terrific! Why didn't you tell me, *senhor*, about the *quinta* where they serve meals in that lovely garden? A *varina* directed me there and I found the place enchanting.'

'But you must also have felt rather *sozinha*.' He murmured the word with a rather wicked emphasis. 'It is the local meeting place for courting couples ... did you not notice?'

'Of course I noticed.' She gave a gay little laugh. 'I expect you sometimes go there yourself, *senhor*.'

'And why should I go there?' he drawled, and she felt his narrowed gaze upon her face as she slipped into the passenger seat. To avoid answering him, she pretended not to have heard him, and busied herself removing the tussore coat.

'I feel rather hot, *senhor*. Would you put it on the back seat for me?'

'You do look a trifle flushed—have you been walking about in the hot sun?' Abruptly the back of his hand was placed against her forehead and the electrifying shock of his touch ran all through her, and she jerked away from him.

'I'm perfectly all right.' Panic made her speak sharply. 'You don't have to treat me like a child who hasn't sense enough to look after herself. If I feel hot, then it's your fault! You bought the coat and insisted that I wear it, as if bare arms are some sort of an affront to your dignity. If I offend your dignity so much, Dom Duarte, then I think it might be a good idea if I leave next week. You gave me six weeks in which to prove myself, and you obviously disapprove of everything I do. I—I can't stay on those terms—I want to go home,' she ended, on such a shaky note that she stopped speaking, in case her voice broke altogether and she gave way to the misery which had invaded her since seeing that beautiful white gown in which Lola was to be married.

'You know,' he said, looking rather dangerous with his narrowed eyelids, and his mouth drawn thinly around the words, 'you should never have left that young man in the first place. It is he whom you wish to rush back to—and don't bother to make a denial! You lunched at the *quinta* and saw the young couples there holding hands, and now you are all on edge for the man in your own heart. So be it!' He snapped his fingers decisively and strode round to take the driver's seat. The engine purred awake and they moved off rapidly through the slumbrous town, heading up the slope that overlooked the sea.

It shimmered through a heat haze ... and through the tears that Rosary battled with, in silent desperation. With every bit of her heart she longed to deny the lie to which she had committed herself ... but if she told the truth he might guess how she felt about him, and that would be equally unbearable. To be pitied by him would be worse than being struck by him!

'You will, of course, stay for the *festa*?' He spoke abruptly, after about ten minutes of silence, and a sudden slowing down of the speed which had carried them for some miles along the headland. 'It will be something for you to remember when you are home again. A fitting farewell, perhaps, to my silver slave.'

'Your what?' she exclaimed, twisting around to look at him with amazement, the tears gone from her eyes to her heart.

'Gisela said it once.' A smile flickered on his lips. 'The night she had her nightmare and I was angry because you were not there. The child said you were not my "silver slave" or anyone else's. You would appear to have infected my daughter with your notions of independence.'

'Then it's just as well that I'm leaving, *senhor*. It wouldn't do for you to have a rebel on your hands when the time comes for *you* to select a husband for Gisela. All this selective mating might be good for the bone structure, but it can't always be good for the heart.'

'I see.' His drawl was menacing. 'Now you take it upon yourself to take our mating habits to task. You, who have been among the Portuguese only a matter of weeks.'

'Does it always work, *senhor*, to marry from the head rather than from the heart?'

'To be ruled by the heart can be a mistake.' He spoke with sudden harshness and suddenly the needle on the speedometer was swinging from fifty to sixty, and up into the seventies. The knuckles of Duarte's hands stood out like porcelain under the brown skin and the car sped along so fast that the sea below the narrow road was a dazzling blur. Rosary flung out a hand and gripped the handle of the door beside her, and she had fearful visions of the car hurtling off the edge of the road.

'I'd rather like to get home to my grandfather in one piece,' she gasped. 'Really! There should be a law against quick-tempered men who drive!'

As she spoke the tall gates of the *palacete* loomed ahead of them, and to her relief the needle began to fall back on the speedometer and as they turned in between the gates he said in a low, threatening voice: 'Miss Bell, I beg of you to stay out of my way during the rest of your stay on Vozes do Mar. The next time we are alone I shall not be responsible for my actions.' The car pulled in smoothly beside the front steps and even as the engine cooled, he gestured curtly at the door beside Rosary. 'Please leave me! I am not coming in!'

She opened the door and slipped out of the car. 'Thanks for the lift,' she said flippantly, and she ran up the steps and along the terrace, not pausing to collect her coat and her dress box. He would have them brought to her later on by one of the maids; right now she wanted only to obey his injunction that she stay out of his way. She heard the car start up, reverse and go off down the drive where it turned into the small lane that led to the Cortez villa. Rosary tried not to feel hurt or envious, but the blessed numbness was gone and all she could think of as she ran upstairs to the cool, calm sanity of her bedroom was that she had no place at all in his life. He had thrust her out very finally with those last few words.

'Stay out of my way ... or I shall not be responsible for my actions.'

His annoyance with her had turned to actual dislike, and to wipe her from his mind he had gone to Lola ... right now he would be holding the Latin girl in his arms, soothed by the velvety murmur of her voice. Like all men he wanted flattery and not the sting of truth, especially when it was delivered by an English girl in his employ. Rosary couldn't suppress a shiver as she remembered the hard grip of his hands on the wheel of the car, the taut control of his face when he had told her to leave him.

Tiredly she kicked off her shoes and walked through the soft pile of the carpet to her bed. She lay there, staring at the ceiling with eyes that ached from too much sunshine, and the effort not to cry. The clock ticked softly beside her bed, and each minute was ticking her out of the *palacete*, off the island, and back home to Surrey. How strange its green hills would seem after the sun-baked sands, and vine-clad terraces of Vozes do Mar. How awful it would be to wake each morning to a day that did not hold one or two glimpses of a tall, dark, impeccably clad man whose sardonic smile she had grown to love so much.

She stared at the revolving shadow of the fan, like the waving legs of a giant insect, and in a while the movements acted like a narcotic and she fell asleep ... to awaken suddenly in darkness some hours later. Even as she sat up her bedroom door was thrust open, the light was switched on and Gisela was running eagerly to her bemused figure on the bed, full of the picnic and her new friends ... swooping on the dress box the maid had brought to Rosary's room and clamouring for it to be opened so that she might see the new dress.

'I can't wait for the *festa*, can you?' Gisela played with the bow that tied the box, and her eyes shone. 'I shall wear the traditional costume which belonged to my mother when she was my age. It's all so exciting and there will be so many people there. You will love it, Rosary!'

'I'm sure I shall.' Rosary spoke with a little touch of irony that was lost on the younger girl ... and then she caught her breath as she realized that Gisela knew nothing of the marriage announcement that would surely be made at the *festa*. It would come as a shock for Gisela, and Rosary could only suppose that Dom Duarte considered this the best way to deal with the problem of letting his daughter know that he was taking a second wife. The excitement and the gaiety would soften the blow; make it seem part of the festivities, a happy thing that would enrich both their lives.

'May I?' Gisela pulled off the bow and lifted the lid of the box. She took the dress from its soft wrappings and gave a gasp of delight. 'You will look beautiful in this, Rosary! You will outshine all the other girls with your silvery hair and your white skin. Every young man will want to make love to you.'

Rosary had to laugh. 'I'm glad you like my fine feathers, but I'm sure I shall not outshine Lola. She is a stunning person, with those big dark eyes and that glossy black hair.'

'She's no different from other Latin girls ... except my mother, who was really beautiful.' Gisela tossed her head, and cold fingers clutched at Rosary's heart. 'Tia Azinha's friends remarked that Lola is wearing a betrothal bracelet of engraved gold, which must mean that she has found a rich man for herself. Everyone knows that she wants a rich and important husband ... I was always afraid that she was after my father, the way she was always cooing over him.'

'Gisela ...' Rosary bit her lip. 'You like Lola, don't you?'

'Not particularly.' The girl stroked the silk of Rosary's dress. 'I much prefer Dacio. He's far more honest ... he's rather like you, Rosary. He says what is in his mind, but Lola only smiles and—and looks sort of like a cat who has licked the cream.'

The description was so apt, but Rosary had never felt less like smiling. Dom Duarte couldn't think of springing on his daughter the fact that he was marrying Lola ... yet what could she do about it? The very thought of speaking to him on such an intimate matter made her flinch ... stay out of my way, he had ordered, and she must do so, and hope to heaven that Gisela would accept the inevitable fact that he was the important man whom Lola was to marry.

'Do hurry, *festa* day!' Gisela danced across the carpet of Rosary's bedroom and with a laugh of happy anticipation she bowed herself out of the room.

# CHAPTER TEN

THE grounds of the wine *quinta* owned by the Ronda family were so overflowing with people that it was like a country fair, this *festa* that made welcome the wine in the autumn.

Moonlight shone in laughing eyes, the scent of wine already in the vines mingled with the smoke drifting upwards from the big open fires over which the sucking pigs were crackling in their shiny skin. Bands of musicians strolled about in their colourful costumes, quickening the pulse with the music of their guitars. Coloured lights glowed among the trees, and many of the women were dressed in the traditional costume, the full skirt flaring with colour, the lacy, full-sleeved blouse, and the medallion earrings embossed with saintly profiles. Rosary could almost imagine that the centuries had slipped back, especially when she saw the wine workers arriving with their shiny dancing boots hung round their necks to keep the dust of the roads off the buff or canary yellow leather.

The girls arrived with camellias in their hair, and the young men wore their best frilled shirts and dark velvet trousers, and these good-looking young couples made it seem very much a *fête d'amour*.

The day before Dacio had asked Rosary if he might escort her to the *festa* and she had accepted his offer in such a heartfelt way that his eyes had gleamed. They still held that gleam, she noticed, as she strolled with him about the grounds of the *quinta* and they watched the fandango dancers whirling and stamping to their hearts' content. They drank *vinho tinto* together and ate cheese and fruit from the food-laden tables.

He had just introduced her to the fruit of the *maracuja*, the passion flower. The fruit to look at was rather like a green tomato, but it wasn't at all sour and tasted rather like a mandarin with a hint of raspberry flavour.

'The *maracuja* is rather like a woman.' Dacio smiled at her and looked dashing in his black velvet suit that fitted him as closely as a matador's. 'It's a deceptive fruit, hiding its tasty sweetness in a cloak of green.'

Rosary wore a swathing of green chiffon about her shoulders, and she smiled at Dacio's meaningful remark. She knew that just lately he found her a bit of a mystery, and instinct warned her that now had come the moment for telling him that she was leaving Vozes do Mar on Monday; taking the small steamer that would call with the mail and the various goods ordered from Portugal.

He fell silent after she had spoken, and then suddenly he drew her in among the trees, away from the crowds, and the sudden glimpse she had of a tall figure in dark suiting walking beside the Marquesa, with Lola and several of the smart visitors from Portugal walking at the other side of him. Gisela was at the *festa* with her two young friends, and as Rosary felt the grip of Dacio's hands on her wrists, she felt a little shaft of pain quite unconnected with the artist. Soon, now, everyone would know about the forthcoming marriage of Dom Duarte do Montqueiro Ardo ... Gisela would know, and Rosary had to find her and be with her when the announcement was made.

'Let me go, Dacio.' She attempted to pull away from him, but he had no intention of letting her go and he leaned over her like a dark moth above a flower, for there was a flower-like quality to her in the white and pale green dress, with the chiffon filming the paleness of her arms and her slim neck. Her hair was piled into the soft ringlets on the crown of her head, and a shaft of moonlight through the foliage of the trees made it gleam like pirate silver. Her eyes looked huge, raised to Dacio's face in pleading, and her mouth was her only feature that showed any colour.

'Not from this place, nor from the island,' he said. 'You need a Latin husband, *amanta mia*. A man who will bring you the gold of his fire to match the silver of your charm...'

'Please...' She twisted away from him, and the chiffon flowed down her body like a mist, intensifying, somehow, the virginal quality about her. 'Don't spoil the *festa* for me, Dacio. I shall never see another.'

'You will see a thousand more if you...'

'No!' Though it hurt, she dragged her hands free of his and ran off so swiftly that the chiffon floated from her shoulders and was left behind among the trees clothed in vines, at the feet of the young Latin who was so attractive, but not for her.

Not for Rosary the love of a Latin ... she who loved too much the man she had avoided for two long days. Not a word had she exchanged with him, and as she sought among the throng for Gisela, there was a sudden hush as a young man leapt upon a great broad wine cask and began to sing a *fado*, the traditional song of the Portuguese, one of lingering passion and a hint of sadness.

Tears sprang to Rosary's eyes. This was for her a goodbye song, a lament she could never express, yet which her heart echoed as the passionate notes trilled out from the masculine lips ... to die, to be lost in the hush that preceded the delighted applause. The young man stood there smiling, a hand on his hip, and then he leapt down to rejoin his girl, who with Latin grace took the camellia from her hair and fitted it into his buttonhole.

Rosary continued with her search for Gisela, and suddenly noticed her by one of the vinewood fires, eating pork from a plate and laughing with other young people. She looked pretty and carefree in her costume, with its velvet bodice and flounced skirt, and scarlet dancing boots. It seemeed rather fateful that she would hear she was to have a stepmother wearing the costume which had been her mother's. The thought spurred Rosary to her side. 'There you are, Gisela. I can see you're having a wonderful time.'

'Yes ... and doesn't my father look handsome? I think if the Marquesa was a younger woman she would make a play for him. Look! They are going up on to the veranda, where a microphone will be fitted up so the Marquesa can give her traditional speech of welcome to the *festa* and wish upon the future wine the best of sweet health and body.'

Rosary's eyes softened as they dwelt on the young and eager face of Duarte's child ... she might have stayed for Gisela's sake, but he had accepted without an argument her decision to leave. He had even made it plain that her presence had become an annoyance, and she hoped that from where he stood upon the veranda, there among the Rondas and their friends, with Lola close by, he couldn't see her beyond the leaping flames of the bonfire. If he saw her, his features would show what he felt. They would freeze into a bronze mask, cold of all warm feeling.

The Marquesa, looking frail and yet wonderful in a beautifully made prune-coloured dress, with a pale beige mink wrap about her shoulders, and with careful make-up outlining her features and her amusingly malicious eyes, spoke for several minutes about the *festa* and how happy she was to see so many of her friends. Happiness and hard work made good wine, she said, and good wine added a sparkle to life.

After the warm applause at the end of her speech, she turned to Dom Duarte, and Rosary felt herself go cold from head to foot as the Marquesa added that their Governor had an announcement to make, which would make sparkle the eyes of a certain young woman known to them all.

Rosary reached for Gisela's hand and the girl gave her a little enquiring smile, and then returned her attention to her father, who now stood in front of the microphone, which was partly concealed by a splash of bougainvillea, the lovely purple plant that grew so lushly all over the island. He stood there, tall and in command of the crowd, smiling a little. 'Wine and romance seem to go together,' he said, and Rosary felt the wild beating of her heart as he turned deliberately to Lola Cortez, lovely and Latin in her gold brocade dress, with a pale lace mantilla framing her glossy hair. She gazed back at him and her eyes seemed to hold his gaze for an interminable moment, then she smiled and seemed to look at the many firelit faces with a hint of arrogance. Rosary bit her lip, and her fingers tightened upon Gisela's ... surely she had seen that look of Lola's before ... on the portrayed face of Isabela, whose self-love had left no room for love of a man.

'You all know Lola Cortez,' Dom Duarte went on. 'This beautiful young woman has lived among us for several years now, and graced our island with her presence. Tonight, as we enjoy the gaiety of the *festa*, it seems appropriate that as your friend, *amigos y amigas*, as well as your Governor, I should have the pleasure of telling you that within a few days the

Senhorita Lola will become the bride of'—he paused, and his eyes were glinting as he swept a hand in the direction of a portly and distinguished man, slightly silvered at the temples, who stood next to the Marquesa—'the Senhor Mateo de Randolfo, the President of the Nacional Banking House in Lisboa.'

Once again loud applause broke out, and then it was announced that everyone must have wine to bless the good health and happiness of the betrothed couple.

'So that's him!' Gisela exclaimed. 'Well, I must say he looks rich, but he isn't very young, is he?'

Rosary stood there speechlessly, and then had to pull herself together as Gisela asked anxiously if she was feeling all right. 'You look terribly pale, Rosary. Are you faint?'

'N-no. I'm a little confused by all the noise. Darling, I'm going off for a little walk by myself among the trees, where it's quiet. You will be all right with your friends?'

'Yes—but perhaps I should come with you?' Gisela drew Rosary's icy hand to her cheek. 'You feel so cold, like a statue. You should have some wine—shall I fetch you a glass?'

'All right, if you wish.' Rosary waited until Gisela was out of sight among the laughing, chattering throng of people, and then blindly she turned and ran ... ran until the trees gave shelter from the storm of emotion which had assailed her when she saw Duarte place the hand of Lola in that of the distinguished visitor from Portugal. The relief had been almost as hard to endure as the acceptance of her own dismissal from his life. She knew with her every instinct that Lola would have loved to be his wife ... she had accepted this other man on the rebound. Someone she had always known, perhaps, who would give her riches if he could not give her the excitement of being the Governor's Lady.

Finding herself out of breath, Rosary stopped running and rested her slim body against a tree. But for the moonlight through an opening in the foliage she would have been in darkness. She had been arming herself for days against the announcement that he was to marry Lola ... now she was totally disarmed by the news that he was to marry no one. It could not alter the fact of her departure. She could neither stay to see him the husband of someone else, nor could she stay to be unloved by him.

She plucked aimlessly a sprig of trailing blossom, with which all these trees were clothed to enhance their beauty. She breathed its perfume, and heard in the distance the sound of music as everyone danced for the bride-to-be.

But for that distant music everything here was strangely still and quiet. When a gecko suddenly chanted in a bush Rosary very nearly jumped out of her skin. She should go back, for Gisela would be searching for her, but a strange lassitude held her immobile where she was, the trailing blossoms soft-petalled against her shoulders. Alone like this she didn't have to smile and parade a false gaiety. She didn't have to pretend that it would be easy to take that steamer on Monday at noon; to stand at the rail and watch Vozes do Mar recede into the distance until it became a blur and then a misty blank, where life would go on as if she had never been a part of it for six world-turning weeks.

She sighed ... and then stiffened as something rustled among the trees, and a few seconds later took shape as tall, dark and unmistakably masculine in the shaft of moonlight.

'So this is where you are hiding yourself.' The voice was deep, even a trifle concerned, shattering the thin veneer of her composure. 'Gisela was worried about you, so I came to find you.'

'I—I'm all right.' She spoke defiantly. 'Do I have to account for all my actions? Didn't you tell me to stay out of your way?'

'Yes, I said that—for your own good.' He came several steps nearer to her and her face revealed itself as very pale, with that hurt quality which the moon reveals and which the daylight conceals with its busy, brash disregard for love. 'Are you not enjoying the *festa*? I saw you earlier with Lola's brother, smiling and eating supper with him. Has he now found another companion?'

'I expect so,' she said, for never for a moment had she taken seriously Dacio's talk of love and marriage. 'Latin men and women belong together. I am the out-sider, and quite soon you will be rid of me, *senhor*.'

'Yes.' He spoke harshly. 'It is better so.'

'Much better,' she agreed. 'Gisela is young and will soon forget me, though it will be nice to remember that she rather liked me.'

With these words Rosary made to move away from him and as she did so the trailing blossoms caught at her hair and hooked themselves in the silver slide that held the soft curls in place. She paused to free herself and at the same time Duarte stepped nearer to help her. How it happened that she found herself in his arms she never knew, but suddenly his arms were more binding than steel bars, but unlike steel they were unbearably tender.

'Gisela told me you were close to fainting after I made my announcement that Lola was to marry Mateo. Tell me something,' Duarte forced up her chin

187

with his fingers and pinned his gaze to hers, 'did you think that I was to be the bridegroom? Come, be as honest as you always are! You have never yet shirked a truth when it needed to be told.'

'It did occur to me——' Her heart was beating so fast that the words shook themselves out of her lips. 'She came often to the *palacete* and it seemed a reasonable assumption.'

'It was never reasonable.' Again that harsh note rang in his voice. 'You knew of the hell I suffered with Isabela. Did you really believe that I would—no, Lola has never been more than the pretty sister of the man I employ in my picture gallery. A Latin girl well versed in the art of charming a man, as Isabela was. But I was young then, unversed myself in the art of knowing a woman. What a pity that you and I did not meet—ah, but if we had met sixteen years ago you would have been a toddler with a mop of silver hair.'

'Why'—Rosary swallowed in order to ease her dry throat—'why should you have wanted to meet me, *senhor*?'

'Because then I should not have wasted my youth on a miserable marriage—now the years have gone, and youth belongs to youth, and I send you home to the young man who awaits you in your own country.'

'There—there is no young man,' she said faintly. 'There never was——'

'But you told me——' Duarte stared down into her eyes, great orbs in the moonlight, wondering, shining a little, but not daring to believe yet that they could let flood into them the hunger and the giving. 'Why did you say such a thing? You always were so truthful that I was bound to believe you.'

'I had no other way of protecting myself——'

'Against me?' he exclaimed.

'Against my feeling for you.'

'What kind of feeling?' Now he gripped her, now he was insistent, and the implacability of his face was giving way to a look that was almost vulnerable. The mask of restraint was slipping, and Rosary was seeing the lonely man that dwelt inside the commanding Governor of Vozes do Mar.

Her courage flooded back, her spirit of adventure revived, the touch of daring that lay in her chin and her lips gave utterance to a single shattering word.

'Love,' she said simply.

In the silence a breeze rustled through the trees and the scent of flowers was strong, as if they stirred at the magic of the word.

'Love?' he echoed. 'For me?'

'Yes.' She stood very still in his arms, waiting for him to thrust her from him 'I—I didn't stop loving you just because you told me to stay away from you. It hurt, but——'

'Enough!' He said it savagely and with a savage tenderness his face pressed hers and his lips found hers in a blind movement of longing. Held by his kiss, her arms slipped of their own will about his neck and her fingers buried themselves in the thickness of his dark hair. If his kiss never ended then he need never tell her that he was only giving way to his loneliness.

Inevitably, because they had to breathe, his kiss did end, and with a little sigh, half pleasure and total fear, she buried her face in his shoulder. She wanted never to leave the warm, strong arms, but if she must, then she wouldn't do it in tears ... until she was alone again.

'I had to tell you to stay away from me, *amor sinha*. I could no longer be near you and not want you. I could no longer look at you and not love you. I could no

189

longer think of you as my daughter's tutor—you who are so much nearer her age than mine. My silver slave, you made me feel a satyr each time I found myself alone with you.'

'You made me feel your slave, *senhor*, each time you looked at me.'

'And you don't like it?' he asked drily.

'As a matter of fact,' she took a deep breath and looked up at him, 'it's the most exciting emotion in the world.'

'You are so young.' He stroked her hair with a lean, caressing hand. 'It would not be fair—but then again it would not be human, eh, to send away my silver slave!'

'It would be hell!' she gasped.

'You would rather stay, *pequena*?' he murmured.

'That would be heaven, Duarte.'

'Then let heaven be ours, my Rosary.'

The bridal music played among the trees, and the heart of the English girl sang of love and joy, there in the arms of her Latin lover.

### A Treasury of Harlequin Romances!

Many of the all time favorite Harlequin Romance Novels have not been available, until now, since the original printing. But on this special introductory offer, they are yours in an exquisitely bound, rich gold hardcover with royal blue imprint. Three complete unabridged novels in each volume. And the cost is so very low you'll be amazed!

## Golden Harlequin Library

**Handsome, Hardcover Library Editions at Paperback Prices! ONLY $1.75 each volume.**

This very special collection of 30 volumes (there'll be more!) of classic Harlequin Romances would be a distinctive addition to your library. And imagine what a delightful gift they'd make for any Harlequin reader!

Start your collection now. See reverse of this page for full details.

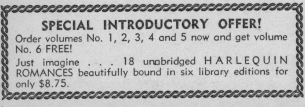

L

# GOLDEN HARLEQUIN LIBRARY — $1.75 each volume

# THE SILVER SLAVE

by VIOLET WINSPEAR

Rosary was confident that she was going to make a good job of tutoring a young Portuguese girl — but Gisela's father, the imposing Dom Duarte de Montqueiro Ardo, thought otherwise. Rosary was too young and inexperienced, he decreed.

And that was not the only problem posed by Dom Duarte . . .

**A HARLEQUIN** *Romance*

PRINTED IN CANADA